Cape Safety, Inc. - Events Won't Stop

Danger Dogs Series, Volume 11

Richard Hughes

Published by Waquoit Wordsmith Press, 2024.

This is a work of fiction. Similarities to real people, places, or events are entirely coincidental.

CAPE SAFETY, INC. - EVENTS WON'T STOP

First edition. November 19, 2024.

Copyright © 2024 Richard Hughes.

ISBN: 979-8230034834

Written by Richard Hughes.

Table of Contents

DEDICATION 1
INTRODUCTION 3
PREFACE 11
Chapter 1 17
Chapter 2 23
Chapter 3 29
Chapter 4 33
Chapter 5 39
Chapter 6 49
Chapter 7 55
Chapter 8 63
Chapter 9 67
Chapter 10 71
Chapter 11 81
Chapter 12 87
Chapter 13 91
Chapter 14 97
Chapter 15 103
Chapter 16 109
Chapter 17 115
Chapter 18 123
Chapter 19 129
Chapter 20 133
Chapter 21 141
Chapter 22 151
Chapter 23 157
Chapter 24 165
Chapter 25 173
Chapter 26 177
Chapter 27 183
Chapter 28 187

Chapter 29 191
Chapter 30 197
Chapter 31 205
Chapter 32 209
Epilogue 213

DEDICATION

At sea and on shore, shown on the book cover, men and women on the job take breathtaking chances with their lives.

Sometimes they feel their livelihoods depend on dangerous risks, and they willingly take those risks. Other times they are compelled by employers, against recognized safety laws, and their own desires, to take these risks.

It has to stop.

No task is so economically essential that someone must risk losing their life to accomplish it.

That is the mission that the consultants of *Cape Safety, Inc.* have long been dedicated to and what they continue to fight for.

Training & educating workers and their managements, fighting corporate greed and general indifference is what CSI consultants do daily using every muscle and brain cell, so that no world citizen is knowingly harmed or killed.

Simply because that level of sacrifice is never necessary for the world's economy to flourish.

INTRODUCTION

In the summer and fall of 2024, much of our main stream media ("MSM") took a turn for the worse when it came to, what should have been their primary objective, honestly inform their readership and viewership, thereby preserving democracy over fascism.

In their zeal for higher readership/viewership ratings for their increasingly repetitive news and political coverage, they decided that this Presidential election would be far more exciting to read about and watch, only if they could keep it a highly competitive horse race to the end.

Hence, the *New York Times*, along with the three major news networks, and its many feeder fish news allies, began to routinely misrepresent the ponderous dialogs of Donald Trump "rallies," essentially writing next day headlines with far saner interpretations of Trump's daily MAGA campaign rants than what had been spoken.

Trump certainly didn't need this help since, nationwide conservative talk radio was already amplifying his hate and plans for a Viktor Orban of Poland style dictatorship, "from day one."

Clear Channel or now **iHeart**,(like most confidence men changing names routinely), was already the country's number-one radio channel owner and leading right-wing propagandist. iHeart's nearest competitor but another right-wing mouthpiece, Audacy, had already been vanquished, final proof that hate talk really sells.

But proof that Russian instigation helped fuel this propaganda came out on September 9, 2024[1]

With 855 stations, iHeartMedia is the largest radio station group owner in the United States,[2] According to BIA Financial Network; iHeartMedia recorded more than $3.5 billion in revenues as of 2021, $1 billion more than the number-two group owner, **Audacy**[1][3].

---

1. https://en.wikipedia.org/wiki/Audacy

This many radio voices and news writers, printing and broadcasting misrepresenting headlines with what Donald Trump never said (but "meant") as interpreted by their respective editorial boards, owners, and producers).

All were desperately trying to keep the American Presidential Election a reasonable two person race by spinning out alternative, unspoken explanations for Donald Trump's inane utterances where *at best* only partial sentences, thoughts, and meaningless gibberish from his monarchial agenda were actually spoken at these rallies, on Truth Social, or elsewhere.

2

These inaccurate headlines and talking points were then echoed by other lazy pundits, broadcasters, show hosts, and news editors, - hour by hour on their respective platforms, becoming the thousand little cuts designed to undo democracy.

But most importantly to them—get good ratings—capitalism gone viral. Daily, these headlines and the programming of our major television networks gave to news readers and media viewers weird

---

2. https://meidasnews.com/news/doj-indicts-russian-nationals-in-10-million-scheme-to-spread-covert-propaganda-to-u-s-audiences

reasoning to the unhinged frantic fables from a seriously demented ex-President.

It was simply to keep the race traditional and conforming to their programming needs. But it was unconscionable.

It was not the media's place to rewrite Donald Trump's rants into more palatable statements, nor was it an honest representation of his daily mainstreaming of viciousness, ignorance, misogyny, narrow nationalism homophobia, and contempt for all non-sycophants.

It was a media effort to present cleaned up Republican policy positions where none actually existed. Broadcasting positions more acceptable for the media's pre-planned political coverage of this bizarre political race. One candidate running for President merely to stay out of prison was being supported by a media completely unwilling to admit that reality to their customers.

Far too many scribes and voices became chroniclers of MAGA's great deception rather than whistleblowers of it.

And all the while the prospect of **Project 2025** (the extremist far-right Heritage Foundation scheme to reshape the Federal Government agenda) was swinging like a blade over the United States Constitution, never seeming to gain a ripple of their collective concern.

It was a steady drip, drip, drip, of political poison.

This was the climate the United States of America had allowed itself to be manipulated into, and progressive companies like Cape Safety, Inc. had been forced to ride this *bull* (at least in language) now for far too many years.

So rather than critical efforts like:

- Leading the all hands on deck assault against climate disaster;
- Fighting against the exploitation of migrant labor to this country and utilizing their considerable skills for our agricultural and routine labor needs;
- Continuing to enhance our medical care and systems in every

way possible;
- Mandating greater safety and health care (new OSHA laws, new EPA laws, new labor regulations, new child care protections) for the American worker;

the S, H, & E (Safety, Health and Environmental) consultants of Cape Safety, Inc. had been in a tiring and clearly unprogressive defensive posture with the American Congress and red states for months, and morale was a challenge for each consultant.

Between the MAGA movement pulling the country back to Jim Crow era ideals; the United States Supreme Court redefining the United States Constitution into some Handmaid's Tale script; and the media losing all focus on what is news and what is circus entertainment, few CSI accomplishments were coming to anyone's attention.

Unquestionably, it was the mainstream media who "both-sided" both the election of 2016 as well as Donald Trump's entire Presidency, normalizing the obvious damage his every action was doing daily to our country and government.

But real accomplishments across the globe were still happening and CSI was in the middle of many of them.

Fortunately, Vice President and Democratic Presidential candidate Kamala Harris knew CSI well and in the past had called upon them often.

So the truth was that during the past 3-1/2 years, in spite of the little public attention the firm generated, President Biden and Veep Harris continued to utilize and depend on CSI to do the difficult, all the while conceding that accomplishing the impossible might take them a tiny bit longer.

After ten prior books in this series it has taken some time to convince myself to keep at it. As you well understand if you've read any (or hopefully all) of my prior Cape Safety, Inc. - Danger Dogs books, all of these books have been written with a dual purpose.

They even led me into a new genre since simply **fiction** as a genre truly sold the books short.

All of these books have weaved a cast of fictional Safety, Health, and Environmental experts (and great people) into situations, circumstances and major events that sometimes never get reported or at best only make a single news cycle. Stories of forensic engineering or construction significance, technological news, climate change advances, new occupational safety/health enhancements, international crisis requiring great expertise, and myriad other—large and small—but nevertheless worthy accomplishments that receive little if any MSM (main stream media) recognition.

Invariably such stories are all but ignored, but if covered once, rarely will they be followed up on. Most of these stories are covered only by specialty publications, trade journals, or buried in the technology sections of magazines.

So it is here that our series tries to fill those knowledge gaps, at least a little.

Cape Safety, Inc. revisits those true news matters through our always on the run characters, implementing their fictional interventions, and usually leaving behind their progressive aspirations for the future.

Not unlike how the *Lone Ranger* left behind his silver bullet as a reminder of his ethos, so, too, do our consultants when they leave behind their safety wisdom.

By now you probably have a relationship with each of these Cape and Cliff characters. Some go as far back as the earliest book and some I continue to add as any two growing firms would need to.

> We've had retirements, a firing or two, a close call or two, and the two founders and original key characters, Bob

Guard and Gene Wing, are only remembered now as guiding stars.

But first time readers need not despair. Prior character knowledge isn't needed, it just adds to the fun.

As I offered for book #10 - *Sawbuck Safety*, here is just the tiniest bit of character background.

All characters are S, H, & E (Safety, Health & Environmental) generalists. The firm's work mandates Renaissance skills, but like all other consultants they each have their strengths.

- Look for the firm's two forensic fire specialists, **Snake** and **Candace** as more and more headlines each month are wild fire-related. A giant concern for human safety & health, and a giant concern for air quality at a time when we can little afford more CO^2 in the atmosphere.
- Fighting for science credibility in this increasingly anti-science political era and keeping the spirits of the workforce high is the role of CEO & lead scientist **Sandra**.
- ADHD, special needs, and legal issues routinely make the news, the specialty of **Sue Mei**, a spectrum gal herself and a strong "hunter farmer[4]" advocate.
- **Claus,** a brainiac from Germany via Princeton & Yale grad is the company statistics, higher mathematics, and AI programming genius who comes in handy only about once every half hour. A polymath who knows his math.
- The gregarious and informative **William** will give you history background until several tide cycles have elapsed. And local Boston history - *"Never Forgetaboutit".*
- **Mike Rocco** and **Lars Frionor** are the owners of both firms with their hands full and each of their forward-thinking minds even fuller.

- Maybe the new crisis, concern, headline problem, or just point of interest, that the firm, "needs the info" on, can be adequately handled by one of CSI's other always active generalist consultants, **Maggie**, **Heidi**, or **Jeremy**?
- Or is the new dilemma, quandary, tight-spot, or Catch-22 in need of the best communications specialists there are? Old-hands **Sam** & **Megan** in Woods Hole at Cape Safety, Inc., and/or **Alice** & **Liza** running the Cliff Safety, Inc. Communications Center, will be called upon.

We've teased with the old Ghostbusters slogan, "*WHO YA GONNA CALL?*" because, often, that is about where the news source I'm following has ended.

A problem is identified by a reporter then abandoned forever when they don't have enough immediate information to write an upbeat conclusion.

Reality works that way.

Many of these stories are begging for white knights to assist, and our media running away from them to simply find the next shiny key doesn't solve much.

So I have invented two coastal firms, Cape Safety, Inc. and Cliff Safety, Inc., to try to save the day. Sometimes the issues are solvable while other times, as in life, answers to complex problems elude us.

After Book #9, ***The New Guard***, you wrote me that, "too much was still happening in the world requiring CSI's fantasy intervention to close out their virtual involvement."

So I listened to you and wrote on.

Naively, I somehow hoped after just "one more" book of tales, our world would surely have its act together so that there would be no more stack of crisis headlines for me to weave my consultants into.

But my growing pile of new reference headlines, emails, articles, book references, and assorted other materials tells me I was far too optimistic.

If you are a loyal reader of my Danger Dogs series, you know how the series is structured in the new genre of **creative nonfiction**[5].

If you are a first-time reader beginning with *Cape Safety, Inc. - Events Won't Stop*, I thank you for your faith that I couldn't have written ten others if the series wasn't interesting, informative, and entertaining.

PREFACE

I typically **PREFACE** with the latest staggering workplace injury numbers and workplace injury costs, which I hope get your attention. These statistics can never include the environmental costs as they remain inestimable, and I trust you'll agree with me that those collective costs are immeasurable by anyone.

As you learned in Book #10 *Sawbuck Safety:*

- When Boeing can't free itself from safety specific problems how much patience should we have with the DOT?
- When deep sea mining permits are being issued to giant sea extraction firms, who is arguing for the rights of possibly human life-sustaining deep sea creatures to flourish undisturbed?
- Will the energy self-sufficiency solutions at Babcock Ranch in Florida be extended elsewhere in America?
- When hellacious firestorm winds take entire cities, Lanai, on Maui; and Ft. McMurray in Alberta what lessons are learned?
- When entire hillside communities in California get washed away forever by unseasonal melting or devastating forest fires resulting from climate change, how do we rebuild?
- When river banks in Louisiana overflow their levees with rising oceans taking coastal housing along the east coast, can such destruction be prevented?
- When intelligent species like orcas, octopus, and penguins are threatened by humanity's actions and decisions—who is trying to make a difference?

At least two companies that you've come to learn more about.

What cost do we give to never, ever, enjoying many of these parts of the world and inhabitants of it in that way again?

As I've written before, when endangered species like blue whales (6 of 13 species now endangered or vulnerable), polar bears, sea turtles, Asian elephants, tigers, rhinos, chimpanzees, vaquitas (a Gulf of California porpoise), leopards, sharks, and penguins are never to be seen again by human eyes, how do we put a dollar amount to their loss to future generations?

Although the Bureau of Labor Injury statistics are compiled from woefully underreported sources, the latest numbers reveal 2,804,200 recordable occupational injury and illness cases during the last full year in their database (2022) up 7.5% and 5,486 fatalities across all sectors up 5.7% from 2021. The fact that this two-year lag in numbers reflect the most recent statistics available to discuss in August 2024 says about all one needs to know about where BLS prioritizes safety performance. The American Bureau of Labor has surprisingly little real interest in **American labor.**

The total cost of work injuries alone in 2021 was $167.0 billion. This figure includes wage and productivity losses[1] of $47.4 billion, medical expenses[2] of $36.6 billion, and administrative expenses[3] of $57.5 billion. This total also includes employers' uninsured costs[4] of $13.8 billion, including the value of time lost by workers other than those with disabling injuries who are directly or indirectly involved in

---

1. https://injuryfacts.nsc.org/glossary/#wage_0bcef9c45bd8a48eda1b26eb0c61c869_20and_0bcef9c45bd8a48eda1b26eb0c61c869_20productivity_0bcef9c45bd8a48eda1b26eb0c61c869_20losses
2. https://injuryfacts.nsc.org/glossary/#medical_0bcef9c45bd8a48eda1b26eb0c61c869_20expenses
3. https://injuryfacts.nsc.org/glossary/#administrative_0bcef9c45bd8a48eda1b26eb0c61c869_20expenses
4. https://injuryfacts.nsc.org/glossary/#employers_0bcef9c45bd8a48eda1b26eb0c61c869_E2_0bcef9c45bd8a48eda1b26eb0c61c869_80_0bcef9c45bd8a48eda1b26eb0c61c869_99_0bcef9c45bd8a48eda1b26eb0c61c869_20uninsured_0bcef9c45bd8a48eda1b26eb0c61c869_20costs

injuries, and the cost of time required to investigate injuries, write up injury reports, and so forth. The total also includes damage to motor vehicles in work-related injuries of $5.4 billion and fire losses of $6.3 billion.

The cost per worker (each worker) in 2021 was $1,080. This includes the value of goods or services each worker must produce to offset the cost of work injuries. It is *not* the average cost of a work-related injury. The average cost per medically consulted injury in 2021 was $42,000, while the average cost per death was $1,340,000. These figures include estimates of wage losses, medical expenses, administrative expenses, and employer costs, but exclude property damage costs except for motor vehicles.[6]

Quality of life estimates, not included, could bring the total loss figure into the trillions.

Every time I start a new book I note how much these statistics increase. Back in 2022 (likely based on 2020 information), the Bureau of Labor Statistics recorded 5,190 workplace fatalities, an 8.9% increase from 2020 (likely based on 2018 information).

Frighteningly in 2021, (when most of America was shut down with the Covid epidemic) a worker still died every 101 minutes from a (non-Covid) workplace injury.

We must do better. We must combat the SCOTUS, State, Federal, House and Senate law~~breakers~~makers, who are working so hard for America's excessive profit interests and so halfheartedly for working Americans.

We must vote out those State Governors out to weaken (come out from hiding behind that expensive podium in Arkansas, Sarah Huckabee) child labor laws, so that migrant labor won't be needed in America—a racist goal not shared by most. Our youth and future citizens don't need to aspire to sharecropping for future careers.

These are the same lawmakers who want to eliminate rights for women workers, especially their health protections. These are the same lawmakers who disgrace the lives of recent immigrant arrivals by calling them rapists and murderers in conflict with the truth that they have always been on America's front line for dangerous work.[7]

The novel you are about to read, the eleventh in the **Cape Safety, Inc.** series, fictionalizes a small company strongly dedicated to altering those statistics.

As I've mentioned already, the stories these characters find themselves in are based on actual incidents and events. Should the headlines seem familiar, that is no coincidence. My characters are woven around real safety heroes who deserve to live longer in our thoughts than in a single daily news article.

By reminding you of these news items that likely skipped your attention while hurrying through your daily lives, I hope to pay tribute to the real victims of these tragedies and to those who truly did their best to prevent them.

Although Cape Safety, Inc. lives only in our imaginations, the spirit and dedication of C.S.I.'s staff are personified for real by hard-working safety professionals throughout the world. To those actual people I have woven into the body of this book, I thank you for being an integral part of my fantasy and soon yours, too.

As these characters are proud to call you their friends, I trust that you, too, would enjoy having friends like these with whom to trade tales.

Don't forget the machinations of two outrageous dogs, a cat in dire need of an attitude adjustment, and two servant robots that have aspirations to higher AI careers.

I know you'll enjoy the diversity of these headline stories weaved into a novel (in both definitions of the word) book format. No one is discouraging Netflix either if someone there has another format in mind!

Although one dictator wannabee, attention strumpet, with 34 convictions against him, has cornered the news market in recent times, the world's major news outlets need to quit chasing after hate news clicks and extend their coverage to hundreds of more important people and events, even small accomplishment newsmakers like the real folks in these books.

They are far more worthy of all our attention, encouragement, and respect.

Spirit willing, you will continue to find me right here in tiny Waquoit Village, two-finger typing up lots more adventures for your enjoyment.

Feel free to send me your thoughts, but hold the prayers for us humanists, at: **capesafetyguy@aol.com**.

Self-publishers have no middlemen. We'll be talking one-to-one so don't be a stranger.

Chapter 1

Claus Kruger was sliding across the floor of the large Woods Hole Cape Safety, Inc. Communications wall of media reminiscent of the khaki pants guy on MSNBC during election night.

Claus was pointing from one to another screen providing

- direct feeds,
- news headlines,
- PowerPoint® generated graphs and charts,
- closed circuit satellite images,
- a live image from a deep water submarine near the Marianas Trench,
- on screen even provided a scanning view from the bridge of a Black Sea deployed U.S. Navy aircraft carrier.

His laser pointer was bleeding battery power as the red dot bounced from one issue to the next, almost all involving to some degree a consultant from CSI.

A large contingent of national and international media personalities, most of who were well-known to everyone, had been invited to CSI's media day. They were enjoying wide ranging Cape Cod specialty food and drink while following the presentation.

"So as you can see, our people are scattered all over the world, helping clients with their safety, health, and environmental management issues. And yes, before you ask, and I know you will, these interventions in more recent years have spilled into some activism for which we make no apologies."

In the beginning CSI was a single location, two person, firm with only a safety guy and an occupational hygienist. But the company grew over the decades into a large two location firm of multiple trained professionals that worked with anyone requesting their help including governments, people without means, billionaires and oligarchs, even problems happening in space, deep under the earth's crust, and miles below the earth's waves.

By many they were categorized as the *Ghostbusters* of S, H, & E, but the two owners of Cape Safety, Inc. on Cape Cod and Cliff Safety, Inc. headquartered in the former Cliff House overlooking San Francisco Bay, resisted that label as far too Hollywood for their life and death mediations.

One nightly news anchor from a national news network seemed to have a problem relating to the firm's departure from a typical run and gun consulting firm just out to amass billable hours.

"So when does your client relationship morph into something more?"

A couple of the attendees groaned at his apparent attempt to generate animosity between the company and its clients over sometimes going above and beyond once the immediate problem had been mollified.

"No, that's a fair question," Claus retorted, more than happy to defend the firm's actions.

"Those people we work for know from the outset that our goal is eliminating downgrading incidents and keeping them from recurring. Once we solve the immediate crisis, say like the time we patched the hull of the tanker *Safer* in the war zone of Yemen, we all realized that a patch was not a replacement. Now some Houthi officials wanted to keep this as a ticking time bomb, and the United Nations would have been just as pleased to declare victory and vamoose too, but we knew better.

We believed in the environmentalists who said this ship's hull was too vulnerable in dozens of other spots, too. So we stayed on the case until finally the world agreed with that assessment.

As you all know we participated far later than our initial intervention stipulated in the complete cargo transfer to a younger tanker, that in truth, not just in name, was really *safer*. We paid our people that month ourselves when the UN budget ran out.

Management here felt that our presence on-site was still necessary so that is pretty much how we roll. We won't walk off a job until we decide we're done. Staying or leaving a project never rests on being paid or not. Did I answer sufficiently?"

And so went the morning.

To keep the media from occasionally painting CSI as bad guys for their involvement in controversial projects, these open house meetings went a long way toward directness and honesty with the press.

Today, somewhat fortuitously, the CSI consultants were well engaged in many controversy free projects. Unless you were still among those laissez-faire capitalists who believed that the welfare of the world's workers, citizens, and the preservation of nature, was only an impediment to healthy profiteering, that is.

And yes, the world still had plenty of those folks around.

One of the biggest safety related events in 2024, chronicled[8] in detail when it happened, had been extensively studied and the incident analysis was coming out.

Following the *MV Dali* containership allision with the Francis Scott Key Bridge in Baltimore Harbor, it was learned that six immigrant contractors who were—in the middle of the night—filling in bridge potholes, were lost.

Maryland had just settled with two Singaporean companies, ship owner, Grace Ocean Pte. Ltd., and ship manager Synergy Marine Group, $103 million for the cost of the bridge, cleanup efforts, environmental damage and other costs stating the collision was "entirely preventable."

The world was still expecting answers.

At the time Mike and Snake had flown directly down to Baltimore in the company plane and were there by daybreak that day to assess the circumstances.

But little could be done at that point but find the remains and figure out a removal strategy for freeing the ship from tons of collapsed bridge then removing the remainder of the bridge from the channel where it obstructed all sea travel.

The project, initially estimated to take 11 months was completed in 11 weeks. It was an extraordinary example of teamwork between a variety of governmental agencies and private contractors.

The NTSB and the Coast Guard had interviewed dozens of people about every aspect of the event. From the ship's pilot to the deck and engine crewmen, even to experts from Hyundai—the firm that developed the ship's power system including its electrical components and circuit breakers.

A preliminary report on the reasons for the ship's loss of power and steerage was scheduled for May 2025, still many months away. According to a Census Bureau assessment the collapse significantly impacted the entire greater Baltimore area, affecting nearly one million people, so the report's conclusions will be important for many people.

Mike and Snake, working hand in hand with Governor Wes Moore, expected the report to detail an isolated incident until only two weeks later in Charleston's Cooper River a similar container ship experienced another power related emergency.

This time the Liberia-flagged *MSC Michigan VII* caused both the closure of the Arthur Ravenel Jr. Bridge and the evacuation of Fort Moultrie Beach when the 304 meter (997 ft.) long ship didn't lose power, rather it randomly increased power and with that, speed.

Leaving the North Charleston Container Terminal the ship suddenly increased speed dramatically. Local law enforcement was quickly notified and took immediate action to halt traffic and evacuate beachgoers in the vessel's projected route. But despite the "dead-slow-speed" ship's settings the vessel failed to respond to those commands and increased in speed to 14 knots or approximately 16 mph. This speed was far too quick to drop anchors or for tugboats to catch up to them.

Fortunately, the highly trained pilots maintained course and were able to safely sail the vessel throughout the harbor then beneath the Ravenel Bridge toward sea.

Ship engineers were finally able to get the ship under control approximately 8.5 miles out to sea where *MV Michigan VII* was able to anchor pending a Coast Guard inspection.

All involved were grateful that only two minor injuries occurred to recreational boaters due to the ship's unanticipated large wake. Amateur video confirmed the vessel exiting the harbor at an alarming speed.

So two consultants were now in the mindset, if not the ensemble, of Sherlock Holmes; seeking through deductive reasoning any commonality to the two similar incidents that had drastically different outcomes.

Chapter 2

William Coffin and Jeremy Tacklebox had just been given a dam(n) tough assignment. Maybe it would be more easily understood if that was rephrased to a widespread, multi-location, dam problem.

William and Jeremy were starting their intervention here in New England where in Connecticut alone there were 4,800 dams, 84% privately owned, and most over a century old. Only 3% of the dams in the country are under federal control presently. The average U. S. dam is 60 years old according to the American Society of Civil Engineers, even though dams are typically built to a 50-year life cycle standard. There are more than 92,000 dams nationwide according to the U. S. Corps. of Engineers.

According to the same agency, being the U. S. Army Corps. of Engineers, Connecticut alone is home to 54 dams per every 100 miles of free-flowing rivers—more than any other state per river mile. The national average is six.

Connecticut appeared to be the epicenter of the new crisis, but dozens of other states had similar issues, including Tennessee's Nolichucky Dam and North Carolina's Walters and Lake Lure dams.

Climate change, the lack of need for these dams, the lack of maintenance to the existing dams, heavy regulation, and the high cost of necessary maintenance were all converging to perfect storms as tragedies threatened with every new rainstorm.

Over half of these dams were originally built to supply water power to mills or local commerce during the era of industrial expansion. The creation of small ponds that could then be dammed into a regular water flow had powered New England's textile, shoe, and many other industries pre-electric power.

But the eras of coal & steam power, fuel oil, natural gas, nuclear power, and now sustainable wind and solar powered electricity, had long ago eliminated any dependence on river water power.

Many of these dams, however, had remained in place, often leaking, failing, and becoming compromised by beavers and decades of leaf and vegetative blockage.

Fixing them right would cost considerable money that most private owners of old dams on their properties simply couldn't afford.

So the five New England Governors had formed a Board of Investigation as to what should, could, and would, be done to safeguard those folks downstream from these dams that would be badly impacted from a sudden dam failure.

For starters two of the board members, William and Jeremy, had already put into their notes that there were no federal or state laws that required owners of high-risk or significant hazard dams to disclose who might be impacted in their respective flood zones should their dam underperform.

Issue #1 should be new safety notification regulations from cities and towns to downstream property owners. The least the owners should expect is some advance warning.

Next the CSI men identified a need for all states to quickly train and deploy dam inspectors to find and classify these dams. Again, in Connecticut alone the lack of inspectors had left over 960 dams without a present day hazard rating, and in some cases the state was uncertain the dam still existed.

Realtors and potential homebuyers had complained that they were unable to tell new homeowners they were buying into a potential inundation zone when they were now unaware where such areas might exist.

Since the state has oversight responsibility for all dams, whether on private property or not, it was Jeremy's and William's view that this inspection, subsequent rating, and inundation zone mapping was a governmental obligation not something individual property owners should have to fund.

Homeowners throughout the country had purchased these dam-located lots without tough regulatory obligations at the time, and to impose those massive engineering fees on them now seemed way out of line.

Most importantly to Jeremy and William was how rapidly high hazard dam remediation could be implemented.

That was where the safety concerns were most critical, deciding what was essential then doing it, be it dredging guck from a pond bed, rebuilding a retaining wall, adding rip rap, or in most cases removing the dam altogether and letting the river flow once again unimpeded.

From nature's standpoint the free-flow could have all manner of positive outcome from fish migrations, to an emptying of mosquito attracting wetlands, to less odorous ponds, to a general change back to more natural ecosystems. All win-win.

Without question it would be a local jobs inducement as well with an opportunity for hundreds, potentially thousands, of contractors to work in their own Vermont, Connecticut, Massachusetts, New Hampshire, and Maine communities on projects that will absolutely enhance and protect properties from potentially serious flooding damage as close as their own neighborhoods. As the slogan of the Corp. of Engineers, **ESSAYONS**, means (taken from the French)—**Let us try.**

CSI, naturally, had already contacted Senators Blumenthal and Murphy in Connecticut and Warren and Markey in Massachusetts who were all behind the initiative. Other New England Senators would also be contacted to get their buy in for more Federal involvement.

FEMA (the Federal Emergency Management Agency) and the Corps. of Engineers[9] would also be able to provide some valuable help although, as usual, CSI wanted the emphasis on prevention not on emergency response after the downgrading events take place.

Things like dependable attention to removing obstructions in places like the Yantic River in Connecticut, Dudleyville Pond in tiny Shutesbury, Massachusetts, the Winooski River in Montpelier, Vermont, and two rivers in Michigan had already caused massive damages.

In Michigan the overwhelmed Edenville and Sanford dams led to the evacuation of about 11,000 people in the central part of the state and devastating destruction in Midland County. The Edenville Dam collapsed due to heavy rains, causing water to surge down the Tittabawasee River and overwhelm the Sanford Dam. It damaged or destroyed more than 2,500 homes and businesses and forced the evacuation of over 10,000 people.

In 2017 heavy rainfall brought California's Oroville dam to crisis stage and forced the evacuation of more than 180,000 people. Between 2015 and 2018 North and South Carolina saw more than 100 dams breached due to record flooding.

Insurance companies, too, would certainly welcome the "attention to prevention" as they often said at both CSI headquarters.

With so many dams still around, the question is certainly valid as to whether they are at all necessary. Ponds were once built purely in support of fishing, recreational use with canoes, and swimming. Some were built centuries back to provide a dependable water source for livestock.

Water wheels for industrial applications are obviously a need from the past.

In truth, as the Corp. of Engineers has been hazard rating dams in recent years, part of their process has been to ask, "Does this dam still need to be here?"

Andrew Fisk, from the non-profit environmental group American Rivers, thinks that many thousands of American dams, "No longer serve a purpose."

"Artificially elevated water tables for no purpose just create a threat," said Jeremy. "And the fewer of these threats the better. Silting of these ponds and rivers, unaddressed, allows pond water levels to rise. Add abnormal climate change storms and often that's enough to crest an embankment or weaken an earthen dam to the failure point."

William knew that their effort wouldn't be easy with as many stakeholders as there were. For every citizen who appreciated the mission to drain the pond to reduce their neighbor's hazard, remove the dam completely, or change the flow to protect properties; there were as many citizens screaming hands off of their favorite swimming hole, kayak spot, or fishing hollow. Folks were still saying that if it lasted this long without causing a problem, why fix it now?

But insurance companies can attest to basement water problems on the rise, undermining of solid land on the rise, faster flooding with greater water volumes resulting in increasing damages and erosion on the rise also.

Yes, aging dams were flood hazards in plain sight, unnoticed infrastructure maybe as essential to safety as bridges, roads, and power grids.

William and Jeremy would need to establish greater citizen awareness of the problem as they gathered up governmental support, and last but never least—secure funding for this dam(n) problem.

Chapter 3

A problem the country had been dealing with for 26 years re-emerged with the regularity of a Swiss timepiece and Sandra, CEO and lead scientist, decided to put Maggie O'Rourke, their Texas grown consultant, on the case for purely political purposes.

This time in Winder, Georgia, part of the metro-Atlanta area, another school shooting occurred. This time a 14-year-old-child killed two students and two teachers and injured many others, including nine who needed hospitalizations. The boy had been linked to violent threats since he was 13 and the gun he used, owned by his dad, was "according to his father" inaccessible.

Dozens of times, by now Cape Safety, Inc. consultants had attempted gun safety interventions that were inevitably sabotaged by the NRA and their far too many misinterpreting 2nd Amendment allies.

- Jonesboro, Arkansas, 1998 - 5 dead, 10 wounded, shot by 11- and 13-year-old boys using nine guns and 2,000 rounds ammunition taken from one of the boy's grandfather's house.
- Columbine, Colorado, 1999 - 12 dead and 21 wounded by two 18-year-old male students using four guns.

Those were the two big shootings everyone remembers from the 25 years of blood spilled in American schools by children and young men firing guns at school children.

But forgotten by most of us are two shootings from 1997, one in Pearl, Mississippi, when a 16 year-old boy killed two students and wounded seven others, and the case in Paducah, Kentucky, when a 14 year old boy used a gun to kill three high school students and wound five more.[10]

Maggie was heading to Georgia to meet again with, tragically still a minority of, Georgia's political leaders on the side of safety to see if there was any way to enhance some of the weakest gun laws in the country. In Georgia presently, there were no background checks, no waiting periods, assault weapon restrictions, no red flag laws, no restrictions to weapons or ammunition ownership, no safety training requirements, no anti-gun kit or ghost gun laws, no gun/ammo seller requirements, open carry was O.K., essentially nothing to keep mayhem out of the hands of the mentally challenged who are willing to use these weapons against their fellow man.

Since the Governor, Brian Kemp, signed a bill into law (Senate Bill 312) essentially allowing unrestricted gun ownership and use, there have been 13 mass shootings in Georgia in the first eight months of 2024.

So that bill has been a real winner, winner, chicken dinner.

In Georgia, a youngster is not allowed to buy Sudafed[11] for his nasal congestion, or a cigarette to sneak in the boy's room. But even a mentally-challenged youngster with a history of threats and violence to others who might be the biggest thug in his reform school, can buy an AR-15 assault weapon with unlimited ammunition as well as any other rifle or handgun as backup.

The Atlanta Journal-Constitution

Georgia mass shootings in 2024

More than a dozen mass shootings have occurred in Georgia during 2024. The Gun Violence Archive defines a mass shooting as any episode in which at least four people are wounded or killed, even if some or all the victims survived. The GVA does not include the shooter in its count. Zoom and click for a description of each incident.

Instead, how about finding something that might reverse this epidemic to turn into a bill, Governor Kemp?

To safety professionals the situation was unfathomable.

Ever since the Supreme Court decided that individual Americans, not just the "well regulated militia" that the Second Amendment references, have a right to "keep and bear arms," our vulnerability to gun violence has exploded. How the country became uniquely captivated and controlled by gun ownership was both a marketing fascination and moral disgrace[12], but it was unassailably true with 120 guns for every 100 Americans now out there in our 50 states.

No one at CSI or even the United States government had the realistic expectation of ever returning the Genie to the bottle and becoming a country as disarmed as every other country on the planet.

That ship had sailed.

But certainly, America can still be doing things to reduce the amount of weaponry easily accessed by the wrong people.

That wasn't beyond the realm of reason and CSI was nothing if not relentless when it came to better safety management and equipment initiatives.

Georgia was not a cesspool of ignorance or apathy. Atlanta was a highly regarded internationally recognized Olympics sponsoring city with several centers of academic excellence and a long list of brilliant favorite sons and daughters.

So Maggie had plenty of allies in Georgia who likewise were pleading for gun violence solutions and regulatory help. They simply were not the same people who had the reins of state and local government at the moment[13].

Maggie would not only need to develop specific recommendations, she would also need to join with those Georgians out to change hearts, minds, and votes.

One thing was certain. It would take a lot more than the vapid "thoughts and prayers" the unrestricted pro-gun crowd passed off as antidotes.

Chapter 4

It was nothing designed on an organizational chart, it just evolved that William, who had a photographic memory for regional history, places, and events had become more of a localized consultant and less of a traveler.

Oh, he had his time when Cliff Safety, Inc. first opened in San Francisco and he was assigned out there for a while. As the Beach Boys sang about the west coast girls, "with that sun shine they all get so tanned." It was an observation he had made himself when he was there and even got serious with a starlet or two.

But eventually he worked his way back to Cape Cod and many of his earliest haunts. As for the future, he was pliable.

When he first started with the company he even had what they all called "his paper route."

In the company van he'd scour the New England coast where local fishermen had begun collecting fishing nets, lobster line, rope hawsers, and all manner of used tie-off equipment for recycling.

William would travel to harbors in P'Town, Chatham, Scituate, Boston, then north to Gloucester, Salem and Rockport then further north to those two *lesser* coastal states as he derided New Hampshire and Maine. Plastic recycling technology had grown so dramatically in the past few years that now the materials could be turned back into myriad new plastic products unidentifiable from their first life as sea lines.

William was also instrumental in the beginning of a Massachusetts-based food to energy plant that was now going countrywide; and lots of other regional S, H, & E "salvation missions" as he called them.

So it was predictable that William's holographic assistant today, in the form of quick stepping Bruno Mars, informed him that he had been assigned a quick local task of checking out a local initiative to recycle used oyster shells helping to save the ocean and reduce waste.

Something, if scalable, that could be extended into the Gulf and West Coasts, maybe even coastline restaurants worldwide.

CSI had been asked to drop by and learn about their Massachusetts Oyster Project activities. William understood that it was primarily because of CSI's notoriously extensive contact list and communications systems.

One good word from CSI would reach literally thousands of existing, former, and even want-to-be customers, in every corner of the globe (sometimes even in space and deep in the ocean where no corners existed).

So if a program wanted to reach worldwide attention, any positive mention by CSI was the way to get it.

The effort was a similar initiative to the plastic rope collection but this coalition of public and nonprofit partners on the Cape was collecting used oyster shells from restaurants then helping to save the ocean with them plus reduce waste. It was a pretty jazzy idea.

William introduced himself to Erica Smith, the Massachusetts Oyster Project Manager, while she and William were standing in the Wellfleet Landfill and staring at two 5-foot tall piles of spent oyster shells.

The Wellfleet Recycling Center was a mere holding area for the 25,000 lbs. of bivalves that had been shucked and sucked, seemingly with no further use.

But into the picture stepped Erica and her group with a fabulous environmental alternative to crushing them for what everyone understands to be an odorific month or two prior to its utilitarian service as a crushed shell driveway somewhere, usually on Cape Cod.

Her alternative was part of a growing effort to divert organic matter such as food byproducts from the state's overburdened food waste stream.

After letting them "rest" here in a pile in Wellfleet where the shells could aerate and become bacteria free through both the hot sun and routine rain, they are then returned to the waters of Cape Cod, creating ideal oyster habitats to clean up the ocean. So far Erica's forces were collecting shells daily from roughly 25 area restaurants and her efforts were expanding.

The aged shells (called cultch) are deposited in Wellfleet Harbor and Yarmouth's Bass River now, creating new habitat for juvenile oysters, which grow on hard substrate such as rock or shell.

So far the program had diverted more than 92,000 pounds of organic matter from the trash in only three years.

William was taking copious notes on the process for dissemination to Gulf and West Coast friends from California to British Columbia. Oysters were consumed on every coast.

Erica Smith was a figurative fountain of information on all things oyster so William simply let her talk while he wrote his key points on his reMARKABLE tablet. He'd print them all out later.

William was learning that due to several environmental conditions each coastal region produced oysters unique in both look and taste.

Once Erica started her comparison all William could do was keep taking notes. She rivaled him for storytelling stamina.

"From Pacific Ocean waters spanning from Alaska down to Chile, oysters farmed in this region tended to run on the smaller side compared to their eastern counterparts.

Yes, these bite-sized bivalve mollusks still pack plenty of flavor.

Within the category of West Coast oysters, you'll find a range of options, from Washington's Kumamoto oysters to Drakes Bay, Marin Coast, and Hog Island oysters gathered in bays along California. West Coast oysters offer clean, fresh flavors with fruitier tasting notes and plump, creamy textures in each bite. As a generalization, West Coast oysters are known for their mildly briny and savory tastes, as warmer waters and reduced salinity levels tend to impact the oysters' overall flavor profile. When placed next to oysters collected from the East Coast, you'll also notice a difference in shell size and cup depth.

East Coast oysters can be farmed along the Atlantic Ocean and the Gulf of Mexico. With a noticeably larger appearance, the shells of fleshy oysters taken from the East Coast are usually in a teardrop shape, and the exterior of the shell itself is smooth.

Once shucked, these morsels offer a robust, salty, and mildly nutty flavor.

Oysters collected in frigid New England waters often take longer to mature and present a more textured, if not sharp, saline flavor.

From the buttery Chesapeake oysters to the briny mid-Atlantic varieties, the length of oyster maturation will also impact the taste. Within the category of East Coast oysters, the firm, briny Atlantic oysters and the mineral Belon[14] or European flats tend to dominate menus.

William, if you're looking for meatier morsels, oysters taken from the East Coast are equally suited for serving on half-shell platters as they are for being cooked on the grill."

Wow, she knew her stuff, thought William.

William had not been an oyster gourmet up to now but the more he was learning the more he thought that being a regional oyster expert could have advantages.

Maybe not specifically to his S, H, and E curriculum vitae but to his restaurant sophistication with the ladies.

"Eating oysters can be compared to wine tasting, sampling cheese, or sipping on whiskies from different parts of the world. The tasting notes of oysters can be separated and identified according to their flavor profiles, textures, and finishes, and the region in which oysters mature will impact the overall experience.

Known as merroir, oysters' unique flavors can depend on a host of variables including water temperature, salinity, and water quality.

While most meaty East Coast oysters generally offer simpler and more straightforward flavor profiles, the smaller West Coast varieties can present layers of briny, fruity, and complex notes for oyster lovers.

Just as you would sample wine varieties, trying different kinds of oysters can help you familiarize yourself with the various tasting profiles and identify which ones you prefer. From saltier, more mineral flavors to sweeter, creamier, and buttery notes, East and West Coast oysters offer plenty of culinary territory to explore."

Although it wouldn't make a difference to any oyster bed rejuvenation efforts, East and West Coast oysters, she showed him, look different since the aquatic environments in which oysters mature impact the size and appearance of both the shells and the meat within.

"Whether waters are filled with flowing seaweed or crashing waves in a more distressing environment, these characteristics can be seen before the oyster is split in two.

East and West Coast oysters can generally be identified by their shape. A smaller, rounder, and more textured shell is characteristic of West Coast oysters, while East Coast oysters have larger teardrop-shaped shells that appear more polished and smooth. The shells of West Coast oysters are also typically wavy or fluted around the edges. And when it comes to color, the thicker shells of East Coast oysters can be dark blue-green, while West Coast oysters often present thinner shells that are gray or off-white in appearance.

Depending on the dishes a serious chef is preparing and how she is planning on presenting the oysters, the differences in shell color and size of the oysters themselves can impact the recipes they are presenting.

As to taste, East Coast oysters are chewy, West Coast oysters are creamy. Oysters growing in nutrient-dense waters develop a plumper texture than those that reach maturation in colder wasters. East Coast oysters are a perfect example, as these bites are more firm and springy than their West Coast counterparts. The meat's texture can make a noticeable difference if you're planning on frying or grilling oysters. Though varying consistencies may go unnoticed by the oyster-tasting novice, East and West Coast oysters can present very different mouth feels. West Coast oysters are often creamy and buttery and offer a texture that's similar to custard. For those wanting a chewier experience, however, East Coast oysters often delivers a more solid, almost meaty texture that takes more effort to bite down on and swallow."

William was overwhelmed with oyster knowledge, most of it unnecessary but all of it interesting. The next time he had a chance to order oysters Rockefeller he'd jump at it.

But now back to the office to write up his report on a successful waste stream reduction and rejuvenation practice that should be scalable throughout the three coasts and honestly much of the Canadian coastline as well.

Keep the shells out of the food waste streams and landfills then offer the shells as ocean protection to the new oyster spat and seed. More folks fed (albeit generally the well-to-do oyster eating folks) with better waste management.

Not a big victory for CSI's environmental efforts but, four singles will equal a run.

Chapter 5

Mike and Lars, the owners of CSI/East and CSI/West, were together for the first time in about a week. Although they always conversed several times a day on company matters via some high technology communications aid it was still essential in their view to get together face to face when important company decisions were under consideration.

This could be one of those meetings.

Since 1981 when the original owners of CSI packed their suitcases and travelled to the deadly Kansas City Hyatt Hotel skywalk collapse to learn what happened, CSI had been in the middle of nearly all major forensic engineering investigations.

It was an effort to turn the unknown into the known but in their case, particularly, to get the reasons for the tragedy into the systems of similarly exposed clients, and others, as soon as possible. It was a nuanced difference from many others with either a vested interest or simply a general interest about the event.

✓ Regulators and governmental authorities needed the information to consider law changes.

✓ Standards people needed the information to consider if changes to their standards were needed.

✓ Victim's families needed the information to get a degree of mental health closure.

✓ Lawyers needed the information to represent various parties in interminable litigation.

✓ Responsible parties needed the information to answer for the cause(s).

✓ The media needed the information to write stories.

The list could probably go longer.

But many of these parties could afford to wait the lengthy time it would take to obtain all the facts, or more accurately, all the facts obtainable.

And it was always lengthy, sometimes years lengthy.

Inevitably too, the "official reports" whether they came from Building Inspection Departments, NFPA[15], Governmental Agencies (like the Coast Guard, NTSB, Army Corps. Of Engineers - so many others) International Authorities, Incident Investigation firms, almost always reached the public in a heavily redacted or politically well-edited form.

Official reports usually sanitized for various reasons—some understandable, some not—but almost always massaging some agenda, even a very well hidden one.

Reports with phraseology like "state of the art," "compliant," "meeting standards," that cleverly dodged the deeper truth that pre-incident what (regulatory speaking, culturally, business acceptable risk) was generally agreed to be "good enough," actually wasn't.

The failure, be it large or small, in repercussions bore testimony that more should have been done to prevent the downgrading incident and waiting for every last detail to come to light although important to some entity more often just served to delay action on remediation.

That was the unique difference in the perspective of Cape Safety, Inc—not to be impulsive or to jump to conclusions but to learn as their own investigations progressed and to immediately impart that wisdom to those with an immediate need to know. To prevent any chance of a recurrence from similar circumstances by getting that knowledge into the right hands as soon as possible.

It was a distinction with a difference from others investigating these events.

CAPE SAFETY, INC. - EVENTS WON'T STOP   41

Others had the philosophy that "the damage was already done" so there was no point in rushing to conclusions.

CSI, however, had a philosophy that such events are never "one-offs" or isolated events to be leisurely studied. Rather they needed to be thought of fluidly as the first failures that others quite likely also faced, therefore needing systemic change, and A.S.A.P.

To do that as promptly as possible, every last detail of the initial failure didn't need to be known.

When the container vessel *Dali* rammed into the Francis Scott Key Bridge in Baltimore, for instance, billions of dollars in damages occurred and it will take years of painstaking study to identify what totally went wrong.

Truthfully, it is not unreasonable to guesstimate that the *Dali* will be broken up in some far off shipyard long before the final finances of the last actual compensation check for damages is decided upon, signed, and someone gets the very last word on who did what wrong.

Ultimately be it a circuit board that failed, a fuse that popped prematurely, a wire that some shipboard rat ate through, or simply an overconfidence that escort tugs were no longer needed, *someday* a final report will emerge.

It is more likely that multiple reports with various conclusions will blur the entire event and bring us straight back to paralysis by analysis and inaction.

But to wait that long or anywhere near that long to check out every electronic system on all similar vessels, or to write regulations that tug escorts stay with the vessels all the way out of the harbor, or that the new bridge be closed to vehicle traffic and construction laborers be taken off the bridge during every ship/bridge passage, is folly.

CSI's stated purpose as a firm was to <u>jump</u> to those safety interventions, <u>not jump</u> toward blame or denial of responsibility.

That was what others did.

So today, the two owners needed to decide if they wanted to be business classified as "Forensic Engineers." Certainly a vital and noble designation but one that possibly inferred a different mission statement to the one they proudly and somewhat uniquely carried.

There were other firms that specialized in that type of engineering and were great at it like Wiss Janney Elstner Associates out in Northbrook, Illinois, (WJE to those at CSI).

So much so that CSI often relied on WJE testing expertise and extensive field & in-house testing equipment to be as dependable as their own testing to obtain critical information for decision-making.

Truly, CSI was not out to compete with the elite forensic engineering firm in the country or give the impression they were redirecting their energies in that direction. The existing working relationship was not something either Mike or Lars wanted to endanger.

WJE not only once reassembled an entire 100-foot section of TWA Flight 800 to determine that the center fuel tank indeed exploded from a static spark killing all 230 people on board; but also had unique testing equipment for issues like structural testing and evaluation, materials testing and evaluation, façade testing, petrographic[16] and microscopic evaluation, thermal analysis, chemical testing, metallurgical testing, corrosion analysis, fatigue and fracture analysis, nondestructive testing and evaluation, instrumentation and load testing, and code compliance testing.

"I'm just spit-balling here but if a tree fell in a forest that nobody ever visited," said Mike, "would we care and want to send one of our people to investigate why the tree fell? That could still be the task of a forensic engineer. But a property concern only. Now, if the tree was in a public park where it could land on someone, well, hell yes."

"Or our proverbial school bus full of nuns," retorted Lars.

"Yes, of course, our ever-endangered theoretical nuns," agreed Mike with a chuckle.

"I see your point, Mike. We have so many people preservation places to be, we don't need to be misappropriated and asked to do work that essentially has only economic consequences."

Mike took another bite of his French pastry. He'd have to remember to compliment Sweeps even though it was simply like thanking Alexa for a playlist.

"WJE, for instance, did a massive project for the St. Louis iconic Gateway Arch just based on some steel discoloration that got someone's attention.

No injuries, no immediate S, H, or E concerns that would be our normal gateways to get involved.

It turned into a project that had them doing thermal and relative humidity monitoring studies to better understand the potential for microclimates within a structure to accelerate corrosion. It then led to a historic structure report as a planning tool for long-term preservation of the monument. Great stuff to be certain but not really in our strike zone, is it?"

"Exactly," said Mike. "Saving lives and limbs is what we do and pure forensic engineering work could take us off our path. It's plenty necessary work but the job of other great engineers, like WJE.

They have the charter and the luxury of measured analysis that we really never have."

"I'd rather *steal their trade with my eyes* like an old guy once told me who loved watching how his plumber fixed his toilet."

"I like the idea that we'll continue to let great companies like theirs do the heavy analysis then we'll take from their expertise whatever safety, health, environmental lessons we can glean," Lars concluded.

"Yes, then with our Communications Systems we can get those lessons immediately into the hands of our clients and friends," said Mike as he gulped his last mouthful of coffee. "That's where we stand out. Nobody has a facilitation network like we do."

Sensing Mike was nearing coffee completion (a chip on the bottom of his coffee cup), the West Coast robotic assistant and AI consultant in training, West Sweepster rolled up to the table with a fresh pot of coffee and his daily baked pastries.

"Would you like just another half cup with a just baked Madeleine, Mike? offered West."

West was on a French pastries kick recently.

"That sounds perfect, Sweepster. How is your studying coming, by the way?"

In his robotic voice Sweeps answered, "I have just downloaded the contents of the past three decades of *Engineering News-Record* magazine into my database and I'm now editing all safety related matters into appropriate folders for faster retrieval. Thank you for asking, Mike."

Sweepster was more than efficient. He was almost an employee leader, albeit virtually, setting everyone's bar a bit higher for his human workmates to also reach.

West Sweepster high speeded it away to accomplish dozens of additional tasks, most of those, now, self directed.

He could even be seen from time to time conversing with his Woods Hole counterpart, East Sweepster, and exchanging database information, in the same way the consultants shared insights.

Kind of a futuristic, Hal 9000 from **2001: A Space Odyssey** but the predictable wave of things to come.

As Mike headed to his office and Lars decided on his next assignment, both men contemplated their mutual decision and felt even more strongly that their present corporate trajectory was the right one.

Firms like WJE had just mirrored the NTSB. Both had just decommissioned their custom-built training facilities for incident investigations to be replaced by computer simulations.

CAPE SAFETY, INC. - EVENTS WON'T STOP

Both NTSB and WJE had just switched to computer models for future incident investigations. That was an extremely expensive endeavor for the 300-employee strong WJE and likely the government's NTSB also.

Lars knew that both their Woods Hole and Cliff site in San Francisco had little expansion room to ever rebuild a TWA 800 approximately 300-foot aircraft fuselage assembly, or even provide a new wing for incident computer modeling, so competing on those fronts would have been all but impossible anyway.

No, the company would continue to partner with others as needed to get maximum S, H, & E advice to their clients. Too many events were still screaming for solutions to focus on additional revenue streams.

Mike gave the down and dirty on not chasing unique forensic engineering work to company attorney Sue Mei who had been permanently located in San Francisco for some time now.

She laughed and said, "Yeah, I was pretty sure that kind of work wasn't our best use of manpower, too. Glad you both agreed on that. By the way Nike has done it again."

Mike was reluctant to ask but naturally did so.

"What now?"

For decades CSI had an off and on relationship with Nike that never resulted in any true change of company direction or heart toward their employees.

Nike Corporation from early on during the importing of their, initially, Japanese running "Tiger Shoes" they had been a thorn in the side of safety, health and environmental consultants like CSI trying to steer them to a safer manufacturing process.

The Oregon plants Phil Knight was then expanding reeked with dangerous air caused by extensive vinyl chloride (VC's) use, and other plastic resin byproducts with grossly inadequate ventilation or personal protective equipment for their workers. The levels Gene Wing had measured way back then were so high there was even an explosion concern.

CSI at the time had detailed how they could become not just OSHA compliant but a comfortable workplace for workers and floor managers. They were largely ignored until OSHA began to lower the boom with fines and headlines. Nike eventually got "as better as they needed to," in the words of the CSI consultant at the time, mainly to stop the fines and negative publicity.

But Nike manufacturing facilities never became comfortable and healthy places to work. Their conversion from toxic VC's to PVC's, a far safer plastic raw material, could be best described as, "reluctant."

However Knight's recalcitrance certainly resulted in financial remuneration beyond the imaginable.

Philip Hampson Knight (now 86), co-founding American billionaire business magnate and chairman *emeritus* of Nike, Inc., became the face of the prevailing global sports equipment and apparel company in America and the world.

Personally, as Nike's initial chairman and CEO, he was now estimated by *Forbes* to have a net worth at $45.0 billion.

Screwing workers has always had rewards.

"Yes, Nike won't pay wages to 4,500 workers in Thailand and Cambodia despite the fact that they made 22 billion dollars in 2023," stated Sue. "What he owes to those workers is about .01% of that profit and, of course, he's fighting them on it."

"Yeah, sounds just like the Phil I know," answered Mike.

During the pandemic, two of Nike's suppliers, Violet Apparel and Hong Seng Knitting, failed to follow wage laws in those two countries, illegally depriving their mostly female workforce of wages they had earned.

Nike had been the poster child of poor labor practices in the 1990's despite Knight's image-enhancing far-right philanthropy in the Oregon area.

Others firms really adopted the policies that Nike bragged about adhering to for subcontracted workers who made Nike products.

Adidas, Burberry, Calvin Klein, Victoria's Secret, and other brands sourced clothing from Cambodia and Thailand during that same pandemic period, too, yet ensured that their workers were properly compensated.

Yet Nike continued to refuse to do the right thing.

HUGO BOSS after being contacted by a variety of CSI's business and governmental contacts recently had done the right thing and cut ties with a supplier using forced labor, so Mike and Sue knew that it could be done.

"How about making those same phone calls that we did with HUGO to see if we can't shake Nike into action?" Mike suggested.

"It would be tragic if our mainstream media sources caught wind of this and someone asked Matt Damon for his Oscar trophy back for his *Air Jordan movie* where he played Knight as a human being."

"I'll hop right on it," Sue answered, and Mike knew she would.

It was a typical hallway exchange with far bigger problems ahead.

Candace Dew handled everything and usually with a panache the rest of the staff on both coasts highly admired.

Candace and Snake were typically engaged in some fire hazard mission or other but Candace wouldn't wait for a project in her specialty. She was the type of consultant who just loved whatever came at her. In September 2022, CSI had been involved in a multi-satellite vectoring effort to find the culprit who sabotaged the Russian Nord Stream pipelines that authorities were sure was intentional. It had cut off a valuable source of natural gas to Germany threatening that country's winter heating needs. Private forces sympathetic to the Ukrainian cause had been suspected and a personal yacht sailing the general area seemed to contain unusual items for a casual sail but, ultimately, nothing could be definitively proven.

But Germany had just released an arrest warrant against a Ukrainian diving instructor who they allege was part of a team that blew up Nord Stream gas pipelines. Allegedly he was one of the divers who planted explosive devices on pipelines running from Russia to Germany.

Three of four pipelines were destroyed becoming a controversial statement against Germany's reliance on Russian gas in the face of Russia's aggression against Ukraine.

Up to now a Swedish probe had been the only one to accumulate evidence that traces of explosive material similar to that found deep in the ocean at the explosion site, matched explosive traces found in the private vessel of the Ukrainian diver.

To date, no country has claimed any responsibility or any involvement in the explosion.

The possibility exists that this was a lone wolf operation.

Candace knew a bit, actually far more than a bit, about explosives and had filled in a few questions the German authorities still had.

She had just put her phone down when Sue walked past and said to her, "Germany, third time today. And it isn't even coffee break time."

The two hit the break room overlooking Seal Island just as West Sweepster, rolled in with two pots of coffee and a large tray of his French pastries, Madeleine's, croissants, baguettes, and pads of butter.

Any thoughts of beginning their perpetual diets were immediately thwarted.

Dalmatian Runnels was the west coast Cliff Safety, Inc. mascot and seagull dog who never met a bird he could catch.

Today would be no different as a tern and a large floppy gull both landed on the deck on an apparent reconnaissance mission.

All but saying, "Not on my watch" Runnels tore after both who flew off with matching squawks. Another job well done was surely the thought running through Runnels' black and white head. True enough, no one would offer opposing testimony.

Chapter 6

An explosion and massive fire broke out at a green-certified shipbreaking yard in Chattogram, (better known as Chittagong) Bangladesh, on September 7, 2024, when workers were dismantling a decommissioned tanker.

The incident occurred at SN Corporation and has been described as one of the most serious recent accidents in the shipbreaking industry.

According to local fire and police officials, the explosion occurred at 11:30 a.m. while a group of 12 workers were cutting into the engine spaces of a partly destroyed former tanker. While the specifics vary, it is believed that the workers were attempting to open one of the fuel tanks or cut through a pump room when the explosion occurred.

Emergency response teams, including two local fire departments, arrived quickly and managed to control the fire. All 12 workers were taken to a nearby hospital. Later on Saturday, eight of the workers with severe burns were moved to an advanced burn unit.

Unfortunately, the yard's 38-year-old manager died from his injuries before arriving at the medical facility. The remaining seven workers have burns on 25 to 80 per cent of their bodies, as well as inhalation issues and hearing loss.

In response to the incident, Bangladesh's Ministry of Industries has ordered an immediate suspension of all operations at the yard and announced the formation of an investigative board to determine the cause of the explosion.

According to a Bangladesh Ship Breakers and Recyclers Association representative, the SN Corporation is one of only four shipbreaking yards in Bangladesh that have been certified as green yards. The organization's initial investigation indicated that all dismantling records were in order at the time of the accident.

However, a union representative stated that the explosion was caused by a failure to adhere to safety regulations, citing insufficient enforcement of workplace safety rules. They claimed contractors hired to perform the cutting work often fail to comply with required safety standards.

Bangladesh's shipbreaking industry has encountered major obstacles in recent years, worsened by the COVID-19 outbreak and the country's economic crisis. Before these incidents, the industry had around 150 operational yards, but numbers dropped to 10-15 yards during the financial crisis.

Despite these obstacles, there has been a comeback, with 30 to 35 yards currently operational, just four of which are green-certified. An additional five to six yards are currently undergoing certification.

According to government data collected by the Labour Resource and Support Center, 124 workers died in accidents at Bangladeshi shipbreaking yards in the past nine years.

According to the Dhaka Tribune, 12 accidents occurred during the first half of 2024, resulting in 12 injuries and one death.

The NGO Shipbreaking Platform, which monitors conditions in Southeast Asia's shipbreaking industry, has criticized operations in Bangladesh, India, and Pakistan.

According to the organization, the industry lacks transparency, and many incidents are likely to go unnoticed.

In its second quarter 2024 report, the NGO stated that Bangladesh dismantled 48 of 94 ships worldwide between April and June, making it the most active country in the industry.

Industry experts and stakeholders are urging for stricter enforcement of safety regulations and increased transparency to prevent such accidents.

CSI had been working on this issue for years. Economically these countries have been exploiting workers and the environment for decades and international shipowners have been their sponsors. These beaches, not "shipyards" as one recognizes a shipyard to be, had never been the place to break ships with resulting fuel and other liquid discharges simply running free into the sand and oceans, yet no country could effectively control the myriad and often well disguised shipowners from striking deals for the millions of dollars of scrap steel each ship hulk represented.

These beaches were not "the only port in a storm" for getting rid of an old ship as these owners frequently lamented to the gullible press and public.

Far from it.

When public pressure from American Navy veterans landed on the United States Navy for allowing their historic vessels to be eliminated by wretched workers in sandals and loincloths on far off beaches, stripping these ships like crows on road kill, changes were made.

Not perfect changes but changes for the better.

Initially and still functioning in Brownsville, Texas, was a responsible American company that became the first true "shipyard" to scrap a U.S. Naval ship in a respectful manner, completed within a dry-dock where the tons of pounds of liquid and bulk waste could be isolated, contained, and removed with proper EPA, and OSHA sanitation and safety protocols followed.

The work was accomplished by workers wearing proper personal protective equipment (PPE) and using advanced tools for cutting and scrapping.

American OSHA labor laws were followed.

CSI had monitored a lot of that work and jumped on the yard a few times when practices slipped. But for the most part, and certainly in comparison to Pakistani and Indian practices, protocols were far better for the S, H, & E protections of breaker yard workers.

Subsequently other yards, domestically and internationally, had established versions of the Brownsville breaker yard, hence far more responsible options were now available than literally driving ships onto a beach and dismantling them right where they beached.

Now even India and Pakistan had acknowledged that they needed to do better and had begun "certifying" yards with more responsible practices. But the word "certified" seemed to be too easily attached to some yards that truly had made only cosmetic changes to their practices, were still exploiting and endangering too many employees, and were still polluting far beyond what existing techniques could readily prevent.

Mike and Lars discussed this incident coast to coast and couldn't help wondering what happened in this circumstance.

Was this tragedy at one of those yards that truly *had* upgraded, and was trying to be more responsible?

Or did it happen at a yard flying a false flag of "certified" whereby the "certification" was bestowed by some approval mill rather than a true 3rd party certified "green" breaker yard?

For historical reasons, neither Mike nor Lars trusted the Indian government's investigation and report. They had both been there and done that with India for decades.

Was the Bangladesh Ship Breakers and Recyclers Association honest or simply a well named front for issuing spurious approvals to yards that didn't come near Brownsville's S, H, and E protocols?

The economics for short-cutting end-of-life ship breaking, dismantling, recycling of ship components, and the like, were considerable. Financial short-cuts remained financially attractive to lots of people in the chain of ship disassembly and needed to be watched closely.

Mike looked at his list of available consultants to complete a report on this safety tragedy.

Their United Nations contacts would surely be asking them for such a study soon anyway. Mike was just anticipating the request.

Snake had the most expertise after the time he spent aboard the Evergreen containership in Baltimore Harbor after that grounding two years back. He had talked with many major containership companies at

CAPE SAFETY, INC. - EVENTS WON'T STOP 53

the time including the Danish shipping company Maersk and felt that he had a sympathetic ear or two there. Frankly, if Snake could convince the biggest shipper in the world to only use truly certified green yards with their end-of-service fleet, the entire ship scrapping industry would experience a real "not being punny[17] here sea change," said Mike to Lars.

But Maersk was an outlier on several fronts in terms of being a good global citizen. Despite a call for an arms embargo by the highest court in the world, Maersk has quietly shipped millions of dollars worth of deadly weapons, fueling Israel's murderous assaults in Gaza.

Without Maersk and other transportation giants, Israel's war machine would grind to a halt. That would be a good thing.

Maersk claimed to be a human rights leader and boasts about adhering to international law.

It wasn't true.

And Maersk isn't just shipping goods — its shipping weapons that are obliterating entire Palestinian families. As the largest shipping company in the world, Maersk is quietly enabling Israel's apartheid regime.

This isn't just about one company. If Maersk did the responsible thing, other global logistics giants like Delta and Lufthansa would likely follow.

It was corporate decision-making to do the right thing that resulted in the downfall of the South African apartheid regime. The rule-book is tried and tested and relies on people-power to force companies to listen and act.

Maersk needed to lead the way in shipping and shipbreaking.

Chapter 7

Was it their close proximity (you could actually see New Bedford from some spots in Woods Hole) simple history since the town was in many ways a city always reflecting America past and present; or was it that New Bedford was simply bursting with economic energy; that constantly drew the consultants from Cape Safety, Inc. back to it?

Whatever it was, Sandra Byrneski, CEO, had a need to have boots on the ground there this morning. Particularly, she wanted one of CSI's consultants to meet up with Megan Waldrep, a fishing authority[18] and founder of the Partners of Commercial Fishermen community. Megan was doing her podcast from New Bedford this week and had plenty of safety advice to offer the fishing community.

William recently had action in the whaling capital of 1800 America, so he got the nod.

William was also the firm's Massachusetts history buff and rarely returned without some new historical details to excite the break room.

Since the Connecticut dam project he and Jeremy had worked together on, both had been working solo on projects like William's Wellfleet oysters caper.

Jeremy Tacklebox was up to his neck compiling the newest container cargo incompatibility information the firm had just received following more at-sea container ship fires that had resulted in personnel injuries and major cargo losses.

The Cargo Integrity Group, an industry collective dedicated to improved cargo safety, had identified 15 specific goods commonly handled in containers that could be problematic. These "Cargos of Concern" (C of C) could be handled by containers properly but protocols needed to be adhered to.

The TT Club, report authors, based their "C of C" on years of actual claim analysis and knew of what they spoke.

Issues like the combustible qualities of seed cake, or the hazards associated with cocoa butter or vegetable oils, needed to be as well recognized as the hazards of lithium batteries and ammonium nitrate.

William gave a final look to the full list of "C of C" he'd be forwarding out to those with a need to know. The Cargo Integrity Group was even more important as containerized ships grew ever bigger and ship fires at sea were escalating in scope and danger.

REACTIVE HAZARDS

- **Charcoal/Carbon**
- **Calcium Hypochlorite**
- **Lithium-ion batteries**
- **Cotton and Wool**
- **Fishmeal and Krill**
- **Seed Cake**

SPILL OR LEAK RISKS

- **Hides and Skins**
- **Wine**
- **Bitumen**
- **Cocoa Butter**
- **Waste-recycled engines and engine parts**
- **Vegetable and other oils, particularly when packed in flexitanks**

IMPROPER PACKING CONSEQUENCES
And Timber
Steel Coils
Marble and Granite

It was an important assignment and Jeremy was making good time with it.

William thought that maybe he could use a few hours away from it nonetheless and suggested that he might like to tag along on William's New Bedford gig.

One event highlighting the importance of Jeremy's work had just landed on his desk from a Coast Guard station in Norway reporting that The *MV Ruby* a break bulk ship flying under the flag of Malta (the most recent spurious country in which to easily register marginally compliant ships) with 20,000 tons of Ammonium Nitrate (think the Oklahoma City Alfred P. Murrah Federal Building, the first NY Trade Center bombing, and the largest man-made non-nuclear explosion ever in Beirut) as a sole cargo *had just run aground.*

The vessel was attempting to transport the cargo of dangerous material to Russia through the Oresund Strait linking Denmark and Sweden; however, the Strait is not deep enough for the ship and it was therefore denied entrance.

Norway and Lithuania, too, had denied *Ruby* entry into any of their ports.

Not only was the ship loaded with explosives, but now it also had a damaged rudder and cracks in its hull.

Its cargo of ammonium nitrate is seven times bigger than the one that caused the 2020 Beirut explosion that killed 218 people. It is the second time this journey that *Ruby* has run aground. Back in August shortly after leaving the Kandalaksha Port in Russia, it had run aground but continued around Norway's north to a dock in Tromso City, Norway, the largest urban area north of the Arctic Circle.

Lots of folks were trying to think this salvage through and Sandra was already on the case providing chemical awareness assistance to those responding. Explosives expert and also a safety manager at the Department of Chemistry at Aarbus University, Peter Hald, said the vessel has explosive power equivalent to that of a first generation atomic bomb.

Dana Piloting had already called off their pilot, and tugboats needed confidence to approach and tie on also.

But for a break of a few hours from the chemical names, and existing cargo incompatibility charts (that all now needed revision) Jeremy answered "sure" to William's suggestion of a break and off they both drove in the company truck, a new FORD 150 Lightning EV.

Jeremy expected a history lesson and before they even got to the Cape Cod Canal, sure enough, William was into a history tale.

"Did you know that the abolitionist and original *anti-slavery* spokesperson Frederick Douglas back in 1838, with two successful escape attempts under his belt, worked as a 20 year old ship's caulker in New Bedford?

Between 1830 and 1834 the number of black seamen in New Bedford nearly quadrupled. So many new people came during that period that they made it a city in 1837."

"Really, that was a pretty significant job even for white workers back then, I think. It must have taken some skill hefting that sledge hammer thing and those chisel tools. I think I saw it re-enacted at Mystic Seaport the last time I went there."

"Indeed," said William. "That tool was called a beetle, and the chisels were called caulking irons and the bigger ones were called hawing irons. Yes, the east coast in the early 1800's had a high demand for men who could keep boats afloat, upgrade all kinds of marine equipment, forge anchors, secure a watertight boat, and a need for coopers who could make tight barrels, sail-makers and rope-makers, ship carpenters, shipwrights, all kinds of ship support."

"Probably the most proficient and the greatest number of caulkers were slaves who learned the trade in ports like

- Baltimore
- Portsmouth, Virginia
- Wilmington, North Carolina &

- Newport, Rhode Island," William called out on his fingers.

"On those ships, tar and pitch mixed with whale blubber were the most common ingredients for hull sealing at the time.

In the shipyards they made these whaling ships, brigs, and sloops water-resistant by putting tar in the hulls. The tar and pitch kept the water back where two seams came together, then cotton and hemp fiber soaked in pine tar was driven tight into the seams with those caulking irons and beetles. As the wood and fibers swelled up the seam became water tight. Usually one man held the iron and another swung the beetle. I'll bet you didn't want to be there when that one guy had a bad swing."

They both laughed.

"I'll further bet that the skilled slave caulkers often jumped the ships heading north so that they could work for pay in northern shipyards," Jeremy speculated.

"So right you are. History says that was the most likely reason Fredrick Douglas went off to do other things like becoming a bee under Abraham Lincoln's saddle during the Civil War. He knew no black man, especially him, would ever get a shipyard promotion.

The white shipyard workers resented all their brown-skinned coworkers, as you would imagine, and didn't make work life enjoyable for any of these former slave coworkers either."

"Sad but predictable," said Jeremy.

"New Bedford was considered one of the primary *maritime escape routes* though, along with Boston and Westport, Massachusetts.

Some abolitionist captains were on the right side and made $100 to smuggle a slave north, others refused to carry slaves from the outset, but the worst were the bastards who took the slave's $100, then when they arrived in one of these three ports, ratted the slave out for an additional $25 from slave catchers who were waiting here for those duplicitous Captains and their ships to arrive.

There was nearly a riot of 3,000 people in tiny Wellfleet on the Cape here over that trick back in the day.

The Protestant church was even accused of not condemning those captains and therefore condoning it. The abolitionist movement wasn't clean and straightforward like some reformers would like the world to think."

No different now with 30% of the country, or so, still behind a madman for President," answered Jeremy. "It's hard to fathom."

"So today we're meeting up with a real friend of fishing, Ashley Blue, who has a podcast that is dedicated to supporting fishing spouses with their everyday problems. Plus she has a wealth of safety knowledge she's trying to impart to the boat crews and captains. We should learn a lot," said William as he pulled into a diner where she was doing her radio guest spot.

Today she was talking to a New Bedford radio audience about an Alaska Sea Grant (ASC) project that those folks and Ashley were trying to bring 479.8 miles to New Bedford.

At least that was the distance Alexa told William.

ASC had just completed a study of 124 fishermen and the top three subjects they desired more training and knowledge in were,

- safety,
- crew and deckhand skills,
- and vessel maintenance.

Safety training for commercial fishermen, Ashley discussed, was comprehensive. But of particular interest and importance were:

- Operating EPIRB's[19]
- Conducting MAYDAY calls
- Using signal flares
- Donning immersion suits and PFD's (personal flotation

CAPE SAFETY, INC. - EVENTS WON'T STOP

devices)
- Launching life rafts and procedures for abandoning ship
- Recovering crewmembers in a man overboard situation
- Skills for surviving in cold water and other in-the-water-skills
- How to handle flooding
- Damage Control
- Fire fighting
- Helicopter rescues
- Dewatering pumps
- Vessel Stability
- Opioid overdose and Narcan[20] training
- Among other emergency preparedness measures.

The safety communication segment, Ashley explained to William and Jeremy, includes a communication to shore plan and proper use of VHF radios that can be used for:

- Distress calls and safety
- Ship-to-shore communication
- Communicating to other vessels
- Navigation including talking to bridge tenders, Coast Guard personnel, harbormasters, pilots, other nearby vessels
- Using the marine operator to place calls to shore
- NOAA weather broadcasts
- Contacting available supplies and services

Importantly, new fishermen (many with only limited English speaking skills) are taught that the Coast Guard only monitors channels 16 and 9, 24 hours a day, 7 days per week, but can track a vessel just from their radio signal. For normal chatter, mariners are required to move from these two channels to another available one as standard VHS radio protocol. This is fresh information to a lot of new fishermen.

Alaska Marine Safety Education Association already offered regional 10-hour and 16- hour classes collectively on these subjects; a 5-hour fishing vessel stability lecture; a 7-hour first aid and CPR class; and an ergonomic injury prevention course geared to commercial fishermen and seafood workers.

They "had just begun putting these training sessions online[21] for other fishermen in the country," Ashley told them.

It would be welcomed and Cape Safety, Inc. would use its two communication centers to relay this information to their many maritime clients and friends.

Sam and Megan ran the Woods Hole Center while Alice and Liza held similar responsibility in Cliff Safety, Inc. on the west coast.

They loved assignments that could inform a broad swath of folks at once like this one, compared to chasing down only a single client.

The odds were far greater that you'd prevent a needless injury by informing many people on every coast and internationally, too.

That was always the wish of communications professionals in an S, H, and E world.

Chapter 8

As sophisticated as this area of management consulting had become over the past 50 years, and it had, there were times when Claus (Yale via Princeton with mathematics majors in combinatorics, discrete geometry, probability, and statistical mechanics) had to remind himself to ditch the advanced knowledge and return to basics.

Much organization management, sadly, had developed and grown their companies without a core understanding that "accidents," a word Claus hated and rarely used, didn't "just happen" but that their occurrence could be forecast and their preventability could absolutely be managed.

That theory dated all the way to 1931 and Herbert William Heinrich's publication, <u>Industrial Accident Prevention: A Scientific Approach</u>. Heinreich at the time proposed a 1:29:300 ratio, stating that for a group of 330 similar incidents, 300 will produce no injury, 29 will cause minor injuries, and one will result in a major injury.

In 1966 Frank Bird expanded on the triangle theory to include near-misses, with a ratio of one serious injury or fatality (SIF) to 10 minor injury incidents, 30 damage-causing incidents, and 600 near-misses.

Over nearly 100 years many people have worked full careers trying to substantiate or dispute both theories but few people deny that the more any unsafe action is performed, the more likely trouble will follow.

Remove a hot coffee mug from a microwave without mitts and you'll likely spill the coffee many times, eventually you'll actually drop it and shatter the mug or stain the floor, and if you keep it up (theory says 330 times or so) that coffee will actually burn your skin and give you an injury.

It relates to almost every action and activity we participate in.

As well, statistically, that serious injury or fatality may be the *first* time you do it unsafely, not the 330th.

So safety strategists for the past 100 years have generally recommended that one never performs the task unsafely, even the very first time it is done.

The result would be never developing a "short cut" habit, or a mindset that, "I can get away with it this one time."

It was simple to explain but difficult to live.

Both personally, off the job, and systemically within any organization.

It seemed too simple an approach to build two world class consulting firms around, but it certainly wasn't.

The AFL-CIO had just issued a report that every day 340 workers died from hazardous workplaces, more than 4700 workers were killed on the job, an estimated 120,000 workers died from occupational diseases, the average fatality rate in American workplaces was 3.4 per 100,000 workers, and the cost of job injuries and illnesses was simply guessed to be between $176 to $352 billion yearly.

And work related incidents were always greatly underreported typically to keep management/worker relations harmonious.

So Claus' broad challenge was to incorporate this theory into as many client organizations as he could in his one lifetime.

There were myriad variations on the theme. One approach was to pro-actively observe another worker at work to identify his/her unsafe actions for resolution before the magic numbers were reached.

Before even the downgrading incident, and certainly, before the minor or major injuries.

The _behavior theory_ had many safety advocates but not usually with management, who resented tying up one worker to simply watch another. Correspondingly, workers were not that keen on the technique either.

People universally resented being watched, particularly for mistakes that a co-worker would then bring to their attention for correction. Some workers felt judged, some irritated, by the safety improvement technique even when it was being offered to make their jobs safer. Some felt it was an intrusion on their work day and an unsolicited interrogation of their coworkers' actions. Some resented it simply because it was, honestly, somewhat boring to perform.

Plus, in an era of worker cutbacks many if not most workplaces just didn't have enough workers to stay ahead of production schedules, never mind cut the staff in half for a time so one worker could watch another and comment on it.

Whether the technique worked well (it did) or not, was no longer the question. The people just weren't available to do it.

So Claus, Sam and Megan were working on AI robots not unlike the East and West Sweepster at the two CSI headquarters who could easily observe a worker at his and her work stations, then, not only make necessary behavioral assessments, but compile these deviations from safe work practice into reports, graphs, and even gracious oral feedback, that was far more acceptable to receive than coworker notes that invariably sounded critical. Claus had even developed an algorithm for a smart clone that could hover out of the way to watch a worker for an extended period without annoying her (him).

These robots went far beyond *Lost in Space*, "Danger, Will Robinson, Danger" machines, and could be deployed throughout the workplace to provide the worker with these helpful assessments with no antagonizing supervisor or safety management intervention. Just a robot to worker safety critique.

It would really become a safety win to not use a coworker's precious time, even a supervisor's valuable time, to give a worker feedback on how they were observed performing their job tasks purely from a safety perspective.

No personality conflicts. Not even the need for management participation or involvement except to deploy the units when called for.

It will be a far better approach to implementing a behavioral management program in a workplace.

Chapter 9

The end of September 2024 saw a new doctrine enter the Philippine maritime community, considered to be the country employing more workers in maritime service than any other.

The Philippines had signed the Magna Carta of Filipino Seafarers, a new law protecting the rights of the country's seafarers.

Marine Insight Press was the first to bring the information to the attention of the Cliff Safety, Inc.'s Communications Center who then had the same information transmitted to Cape Safety, Inc. within seconds.

It was good news and a long time coming. But the two coasts prayed that they'd also live the document as well as announce it.

President Ferdinand R. Marcos Jr. presided over the signing ceremony on September 23, 2024, and restated the law's importance.

The law deals with issues such as fair wages, safe working conditions, and skill development for seafarers.

It had been passed to increase protections for Filipino seafarers, particularly those who work on international vessels. It also aimed to address concerns raised by the international community about training and certification guidelines.

The new law established stricter education and training requirements for seafarers to meet global standards such as the Standards for Training, Certification, and Watchkeeping (STCW).

According to President Marcos, the Magna Carta focused on fair wages, worker safety from hazards and exploitation and provisions for ongoing skill development.

He said seafarers deserve fair salaries for their dedication and hard work and that their working conditions should prioritize compliance, safety, and protection.

The law also encourages career advancement by providing training and certification support to improve Filipino seafarers' competitiveness in the global market.

The law was aligned with international maritime labour[22] laws, ensuring that Filipino seafarers were compliant and exceptional at meeting the evolving demands of the maritime sector.

It also combined efforts from several government departments, such as the Department of Foreign Affairs, the Department of Labor and Employment, and the Maritime Industry Authority (MARINA), to streamline policies and improve the entire system for seafarers.

House Speaker Ferdinand Martin Romualdez stated that the law was essential for maintaining the Philippines' status as the world's largest provider of seafarers.

The law aimed to ensure the continuous employment of Filipino seafarers while protecting them from exploitation and discrimination, especially women seafarers.

While the Magna Carta provided extensive protections and rights to seafarers, it had been criticized for some controversial aspects.

One of the most contentious issues was the requirement for seafarers to post a bond in disability disputes with employers, which could delay the issuance of awards until all appeals are completed.

Despite some political delays in its passage, the Magna Carta was considered a timely resolution to the issues faced by Filipino seafarers, mainly due to worldwide concerns about training standards and threats from the European Union to stop accepting Filipino credentials.

President Marcos stated that the law showed the government's commitment to helping the seafaring community and ensuring their safety.

Around the same time the United Kingdom was making a proclamation of their own after a foreign ship-owner had made a monkey of British Labor in 2022 when they swept in to buy their primary ferry service while simultaneously firing all British crewmembers and replacing them with underpaid foreign seamen.

The UK government had just unveiled a draft **Employment Rights Bill** aimed at enhancing protections for seafarers, a move welcomed by UK-based maritime union Nautilus International. The bill, set to be introduced in Parliament, focused on toughening laws around collective dismissal and reinforcing wage protections for seafarers in UK law.

The bill, set to be introduced to Parliament would outlaw the practice of "fire and rehire" by requiring employers to prove there is no reasonable financial alternative to dismissing staff.

The bill also closed a loophole used by P&O Ferries in 2022 by strengthening collective redundancy notification requirements for foreign vessel operators. This measure aimed to prevent incidents like the one that sparked public outrage when P&O Ferries abruptly fired 800 UK-based ferry workers[1], replacing them with cheaper foreign agency workers.

Under the new bill, vessel operators planning to dismiss 20 or more employees must now first notify the UK Government.

"Ending the scourge of meaningless fire and rehire, a damaging practice that has caused widespread instability for maritime professionals, will be a victory for seafarers' rights and a strong message of fairness and respect for all workers," said Martyn Gray, director of organizing at Nautilus International.

"Ensuring that all seafarers regularly working in UK waters are paid at least the national minimum wage equivalent is a welcome development, addressing a long-standing issue of wage exploitation in the industry," Gray added.

While Nautilus International acknowledged these measures as a crucial milestone, it believed stronger protections are still necessary.

---

1. https://gcaptain.com/criminal-civial-investigations-p-o-ferries/

The union plans to advocate for additional safeguards as the bill moves through Parliament.

"This is just the beginning. We will work closely with lawmakers as the Bill moves forward to ensure it delivers the strongest possible protections for seafarers and maritime professionals," Gray said.

Such actions were one of the reasons why the Jones Act existed in the United States mandating American workers for American port to port transports, and why the union staunchly resisted any (routinely big business inspired) efforts to weaken or outright eliminate Jones Act provisions and purposes.

Chapter 10

Holding a book in front of Maggie, Mike announced, "This guy is *wicked sma't*, mocking his own Boston accent.

"Let's see if we can invite him to lunch or dinner or something and pick his brain about his new book. He could be one important asset to us somewhere in the future if not immediately."

Maggie in her own Texas drawl that she never lost in over 30 years at CSI, answered, *"I'm on it, pard'ner."*

The accents thing was their Cú Chulainn.[23]

Who they were both talking about was Daniel J. Levitin, who had just written a fantastically interesting book titled, *I Heard There Was A Secret Chord*[24], detailing his recent findings on music as medicine.

Music is one of humanity's oldest medicines, he documents, from the Far East to the Ottoman Empire, Europe to Africa and pre-colonial America, right up to the dressing rooms of the NBA where the best professional basketball players listen to music before games for inspiration. Most players prefer rap but the greatest player, Lebrun James, opts for very different, smooth jazz. Why?

Is there any reason to a personal playlist? Does it provide any lesson? Does music, voice, sound(s) affect human performance in any way, physically, mentally, spiritually, that is measureable? Can music heal? Is there a beat, a rhythm, a tone, a timber, to sounds and music that naturally triggers or stimulates the human brain? Healing?

How is music leading to better patient results for all manner of psychological and purely physical problems? Movement disorders like Parkinson's, Brain Trauma Injuries, ALS, PTSD, ADHD, Suicide, Tourette's Syndrome, memory loss issues like Dementia and Alzheimer's, stroke, and everyday pain can be treated with music with some patients evidencing considerable improvement. How are sounds and music being used therapeutically already for certain cognitive impairments, injuries, and birth abnormalities?

Mike, who had just finished the book, now knew that Daniel Levitin was a young neuroscientist, a musician, a known entity to many in the music and academic communities, and the author of four *New York Times* bestselling books with a lot to communicate to the S, H, & E world, which CSI consultants needed to hear.

A quick get together would be a wonderful start and maybe then he could be convinced to be an evening speaker at one of their monthly meetings.

If anyone could charm him into it, that person would be Maggie.

Yes, the sooner the better, please.

A big part of the country was still mentally locked into a bubble of hate and truth disavowance being egged on by a former President fighting to avoid a well deserved prison sentence.

As Thom Hartman, social science observer and writer had recently postulated, "Could the Covid disaster of 2020—which Trump botched so badly that America has had more Covid deaths than any other nation in the world except Peru (whose president denied Covid was dangerous)—be what's fueling the Trump MAGA cult? Are we, in other words, as a nation, suffering from Post Traumatic Stress Disorder (PTSD), and that is what is driving a national mental illness crisis that opened the door for Trump's cult to grow?

Colorado elections worker Tina Peters, for example, was just sent to prison for nine years for her role in trying to subvert the 2020 election; she'd completely bought into Trump's lie that Democrats had stolen that election and is paying for it with the rest of her life."

Maybe music could free their misdirected hate, thought Maggie.

Thom had correctly observed and reported that, "All across America, families are being torn[1] apart by the Trump cult, and sometimes the conflicts even lead to violence.

The rest of the world has figured this out. Over at the British newspaper *The Independent,* the headline says it all:

"She Escaped the Religious Sect She Grew Up In. Now She Says Trump's MAGA Movement is eerily similar"

Although the economy right now was doing better than at any time since the 1960's, polls show a majority of Americans would rather believe Trump's lies that inflation is still with us (it's down to **1.7 percent**[2] now) and the historically low 4.1 percent unemployment rate is "fake news." And tens of millions of Americans believe him.

So, what's going on here in America? How did we get here and why?

Many otherwise normal and sane Americans seem to have gone nuts, leaping down the QAnon or Fox "News" rabbit holes in search of meaning, safety, and explanations for the feelings of doom that they just can't shake.

It's as if some major event in their lives has created such a trauma that they've been knocked off balance, psychologically.

---

1. https://www.latimes.com/opinion/story/2024-01-14/lost-cause-platform-donald-trump-revision-history-confederacy

2. https://www.washingtonexaminer.com/policy/finance-and-economy/3151645/inflation-dropped-to-1-7-in-august-in-producer-price-index/#_853ae90f0351324bd73ea615e6487517__4c761f170e016836ff84498202b99827_ _853ae90f0351324bd73ea615e6487517_text_43ec3e5dee6e706af7766fffea512721_Inflati on_0bcef9c45bd8a48eda1b26eb0c61c869_2C_0bcef9c45bd8a48eda1b26eb0c61c869_20 as_0bcef9c45bd8a48eda1b26eb0c61c869_20measured_0bcef9c45bd8a48eda1b26eb0c61 c869_20by_0bcef9c45bd8a48eda1b26eb0c61c869_20the_c0cb5f0fcf239ab3d9c1fcd31fff 1efc_Labor_0bcef9c45bd8a48eda1b26eb0c61c869_20Statistics_0bcef9c45bd8a48eda1b2 6eb0c61c869_20reported_0bcef9c45bd8a48eda1b26eb0c61c869_20on_0bcef9c45bd8a48 eda1b26eb0c61c869_20Thursday.

And that could be a big part of the answer, particularly given how neither our insurance industry nor our government-funded health insurance programs typically pay for mental health services that might otherwise help out people suffering from trauma-induced shock."

Hey, thought Maggie, it was a theory, at least. Thom had written complete books on the human condition of PTSD and knew of what he spoke.

"Consider some of the cardinal symptoms of PTSD, something that's often brought on by a near-death-experience, severe abuse, or surviving a once-in-a-century pandemic.

Each symptom would make a person more vulnerable to the siren song of Trump's cult:

◯ Hypervigilance[3] and threat sensitivity, causing people to experience heightened alertness to potential and often imagined (like Trump's lies about Haitian immigrants) threats.

◯ Difficulty with trust[4], which may lead to skepticism of official sources and greater reliance on alternative information channels; vulnerability, in other words, to Trump's lies and his claims of "fake news" when he's fact-checked.

◯ Emotional dysregulation[5], making individuals like Tina Peters, the hundreds of January 6th rioters now in jail, and other Trump followers more vulnerable to emotionally-charged misinformation and MAGA cult membership.

---

3. https://www.ncbi.nlm.nih.gov/pmc/articles/PMC8932400/

4. https://www.charliehealth.com/post/can-you-get-ptsd-from-emotional-abuse

5. https://www.ncbi.nlm.nih.gov/pmc/articles/PMC3181584/

○ <u>Cognitive</u> changes impacting critical thinking skills needed to evaluate information that might contradict the lies that Trump and his co-conspirators promulgate.

○ <u>Social</u> isolation[6], which may limit exposure to different perspectives and fact-checking from others who try to tell MAGA members how deluded and exploited they really are.

○ <u>Seeking</u> explanations[7] causing people to have a heightened need to understand and make sense of their experiences, making them more open to MAGA's anti-science and politically charged explanatory narratives, even when they're lies.

○ <u>Avoidance</u> behaviors leading people to avoid exposure to diverse information sources, keeping them trapped in Trump cult bubbles like rightwing hate radio and Fox "News."

Multiple **studies**[8] have been done on the psychological impact of the Covid pandemic, finding anywhere from **5 to 55 percent**[9] of Americans suffering in a way that could be diagnosed as PTSD. The **average**[10] across the studies find 26 percent of Americans having diagnosable PTSD from Covid.

---

6. https://www.charliehealth.com/post/can-you-get-ptsd-from-emotional-abuse

7. https://news.gsu.edu/research-magazine/two-years-of-trauma

8. https://medicine.yale.edu/news-article/covid-19-and-ptsd-assessing-the-pandemics-toll-on-mental-health/

9. https://medicine.yale.edu/news-article/covid-19-and-ptsd-assessing-the-pandemics-toll-on-mental-health/

10. https://medicine.yale.edu/news-article/covid-19-and-ptsd-assessing-the-pandemics-toll-on-mental-health/

Prior to the pandemic, the national rate of diagnosable PTSD was generally considered to be around[11] 3.5 percent. Clearly, the pandemic had an impact on our psyches that Trump has been exploiting every day since.

Remember, for almost an entire year, we were afraid that just going to the grocery store could kill us. Over a million of us—one out of every 272 Americans—died because of Trump's incompetence and malice[12].

Most of us knew people who died.

As the lead author[13] of a new study[14] on the impact of Covid, Dr. Jeff Ashby, noted:

"While many people are insulated from deaths and economic hardships related to the pandemic, there is a universal experience of fear, concern for others, and social isolation. Among our findings is that the experience of COVID-19 is a traumatic stress. It isn't just triggering earlier trauma, it's a traumatic experience in and of itself."

Literally millions of people have joined Trump's cult—it is a cult[15], as its members are so impervious to factual information and it's based on the personality of a single man[16]—and the evidence suggests that many of them may have been made vulnerable[17] to joining MAGA because of the trauma they experienced during the worst of the pandemic.

---

11. https://medicine.yale.edu/news-article/covid-19-and-ptsd-assessing-the-pandemics-toll-on-mental-health/

12. https://hartmannreport.com/p/covid-this-month-4-years-ago-trump-73b

13. https://education.gsu.edu/profile/jeff-ashby/

14. https://news.gsu.edu/research-magazine/two-years-of-trauma

15. https://www.theatlantic.com/ideas/archive/2023/08/trumpism-maga-cult-republican-voters-indoctrination/675173/

16. https://www.scientificamerican.com/article/trumps-personality-cult-plays-a-part-in-his-political-appeal/

17. https://pubmed.ncbi.nlm.nih.gov/8234595/

As Dr. Stephen Schwartz wrote[18] for the *National Library of Medicine:*

"[T]his [million-plus Covid] death rate is directly correlated to the politicization and weaponization of anti-science throughout the MAGA world created by Donald Trump and the Republican Party. . . . Anti-vaxxers, and anti-maskers, usually the same people, have made fidelity to a fact-free but emotionally satisfying reality more important than life itself, and created the first American death cult. . . .

"There was a deliberate plan from the very outbreak of the Covid pandemic to take what should have been a fringe movement—there were the equivalent of anti-vaxxers in the Middle Ages with the Plague; there were anti-vaxxers with the 1918 Spanish Flu—and transform it into a mainstream political movement. What had been fringe became a death culture involving millions. Believers willingly subject themselves to a vastly higher risk of contracting and dying of Covid. And they do this in the face of a million dead, and 2000 people, or more, dying each day.

The good news is that the way most cult members leave their cult is not through deprogramming or a sudden awakening (although those do happen) but, rather, because the cult leader dies or is discredited[19].

Trump decisively losing the 2024 election may well be that discrediting and thus liberating event in the lives of many of his followers.

---

18.   https://www.ncbi.nlm.nih.gov/pmc/articles/PMC8935966/

19. https://aeon.co/essays/how-cult-leaders-brainwash-followers-for-total-control

The challenge for the next year or so will be—for those of us who recognize the cult-like slavish devotion to Trump by his followers—to provide support to those followers we know to make the transition from the Trump cult back into the normal world. Therapy for the PTSD that made them vulnerable in the first place will also be helpful.

America can recover from this trauma, but it'll take time and effort."

Maggie felt it was tragic that on top of the many concerning worldwide S, H, and E disasters facing America each day, having to put down both this Trump Covid misdirection and associated *Trump mind f&$ck* of his supporters, was a terrible bleed of resources and attention.

But the earliest signs of backbone and return to a personal responsibility for one's destiny were showing.

Maybe so many of our fellow Americans had been infused with so much resentment over the Covid disruption that a reintroduction to normalcy and economically prosperous times was too much change for them to handle, particularly if the gloom and doom negativism was more enticing than getting off the couch and moving forward.

Certainly the Vice Presidential selection Trump had made showed a curious predilection for couches, she smirked to a mirror as she passed it.

Maybe the music man was just what was needed?

It was a curious time for America, pre-election 2024.

It was the same in many ways with business fluctuations still causing disruptions to people's lives both predictable and unpredictable.

But again more personal responsibility for one's economic fate was also appearing in headlines.

◈ East coast dockworkers in 65 eastern and gulf ports seeing those ports reap over $400 billion in profiteering in a 3-year window demanded and got their share, when a 62% pay raise was quickly negotiated.

◈ Restaurant workers were demanding laws for at least minimum wage in allowed "tips only" states, and getting them passed.

◈ State ballot initiatives for what had become now ubiquitous food delivery drivers demanding a fairer share of the economic pie.

◈ And far less forgiving public responses to personal and company failures

One clear example of the latter was the Boar's Head deli meat plant closure in Jarratt, Virginia, after a Listeria outbreak from their products killed nine people and hospitalized at least 57 more across 18 states.
That plant was the largest private employer in that small town, and 500 workers had just became unemployed over their collective failures.
According to the *Department of Agriculture Inspectors for Health and Safety,* the plant had frequently been cited for H & S infractions including violations like having "dirty" machinery; flies in pickle containers; "heavy meat buildup" on walls; blood in puddles on the floor; multiple instances of leaky pipes; clogged drains, and heavy dust buildups in many areas. Mold was also visible in a number of areas in the plant.
To the point, it was eventually the health tragedies that closed the plant not employee whistleblowers, bringing most observers to feel that plant employees, as well as Boar's Head managers, bore mutual responsibility for these deaths and injuries. Few observers felt sorry for the fate of those unemployed workers with the closing of that plant.

The trend was starting that with greater employee engagement with an operation, employees, too, held a responsibility to do right for consumers. Maggie saw little wrong with this popular attitude and wished she saw more of it.

Why not something akin to a workforce threatening to strike *if they didn't get a 6% pay raise, and new safety equipment, and the replacement of a nasty man-eater piece of equipment, and a doubling of the size of the day-care facility.*

That might make a nice headline plus some progressive change for the better at that workplace.

Higher wages alone are not always what is needed.

Chapter 11

Snake had a long history of working with the United States Coast Guard in a wide variety of directions they were not designated to go. So the missions they retained were also of direct interest to Cape Safety, Inc.

Also the more difficulty the Coast Guard had serving out its assigned missions, the greater the likelihood that they'd, surreptitiously, be contacting their private sector friends for possible backup.

Not ship engagements, drug interdiction, or the armed stuff, naturally. But often the statistics work, the research work, and the behind the curtain stuff that every military agency has too much of.

So the personnel news that they were sharing over a few cups of sturdy Coast Guard coffee had a strong bearing on their mutual behind the scenes working relationship.

Personnel shortages in the Coast Guard in 2024 were scheduled to sideline 10 cutters and 29 stations, bad news indeed.

Recruitment and retention challenges had led the service into a system wide service retreat thanks to a 3,500 person shortfall in the enlisted ranks, a nearly 10% reduction.

This massive shortage is forcing the Coast Guard to take ten cutters out of service, transfer five tugs to seasonal activation only, and shutter 29 boat stations.

According to Coast Guard Commandant Admiral Linda Fagan, "the Coast Guard has never been in greater demand around the world, but this realignment will not cause a delay in their most vital Search and Rescue capabilities."

Few Americans realized it but the United States Coast Guard even had international missions. Just recently, for instance the cutter *James WMSL 754* arrived in the port of Rio de Janeiro, Brazil, on a scheduled mission.

The visit was their third stop of a multi-mission deployment in the South Atlantic demonstrating the interoperability of the two nation's maritime forces to counter illicit maritime activity and promote their maritime authority throughout the region. Unmanned aerial systems augment both services presently.

Tactics, techniques and procedures for successful interdictions have been shared between both countries since 2009. Normally the *James* is homeported in Charleston, South Carolina.

Certainly the overall force of 57,000 active duty and reserve personnel had already been stretched thin but getting boxed out of a $100 billion funding for security and the borders, will be noticed.

Cape Safety, Inc. had been part of the vanguard that felt the agency could breathe easier if they were given flexibility to simply fund recruitment efforts and be allowed to test out new personnel management approaches.

One area that was allowed to implement change was the Coast Guard Academy in New London, Connecticut. The Academy was now seeing positive results from realigning their culture away from the typical military academy regimented four years, toward a more academically focused and greater self-determination structure for future officers.

Major lawsuits against the school for accepting too much cadet controlled discipline, including sexual intimidation of female cadets and traditional hazing, had recently been settled for millions of dollars. That structure of four-year education was now acknowledged to be out of step with 2024 Coast Guard values and the ultimate goals of the Academy.

But put in naval terms the Coast Guard cuts are incredibly drastic. Not unlike if the Pentagon had suddenly decided, virtually overnight, to send 14 of America's fleet of 73 *Arleigh Burke*-class destroyers to the scrap yard, while looking toward a handful of Nimitz class aircraft carriers, and some lower capability Littoral combat ships to fill their capability gap.

It was hard to imagine that such a decline in vessels would not hurt border interdictions of waterborne drug smuggling, fisheries management, personnel safety relating to increased offshore construction of wind and tidal energy installations, illegal ocean mining, Northwest Passage patrols, and other assignments taken on by the Coast Guard, in addition to their ongoing S & R missions, in recent years.

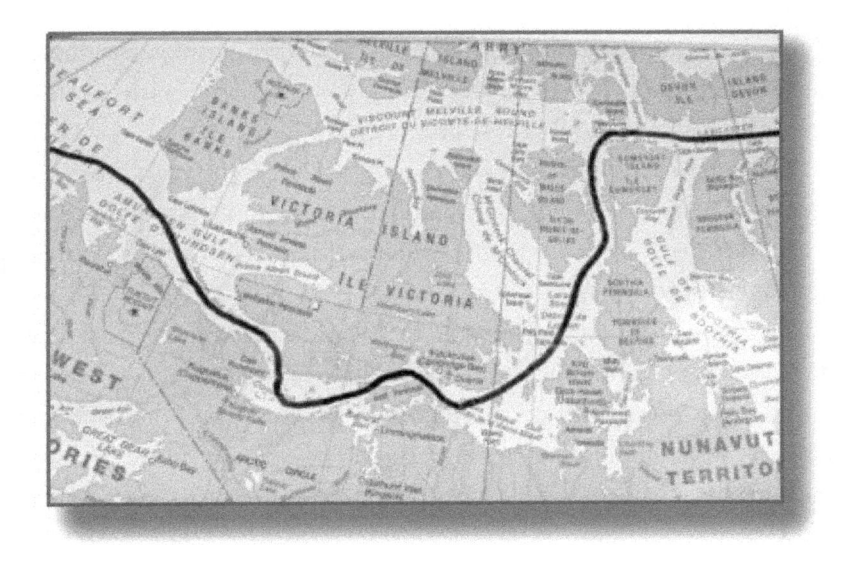

But Snake appreciated that what the Commandant was telling him about these painful cuts—that as much as they hurt, they made sense. The ships being retired, the *Reliance* class cutters, were all approaching six decades of service, and hard service it had been.

The phrase "ridden hard and put away wet"[25] would actually fit all of these United States Coast Guard cutters to a T. Most of them experienced only vital shipyard visits in their histories due to their always *mission-critical* importance. As operational casualties mounted, the Guard simply couldn't afford to keep most of these solid-state vessels operational in a new high-tech necessary maritime environment.

The land-based deficiencies had repercussions also. Many of the installations soon to be shuttered had been operating with 60% of approved staff, resulting in some levels of neglect there as well.

So as hard as they were to hear about, these announcements, Snake had to admit, were a bold response when, in prior times the Coast Guard, like other services, masked these realities with further short-staffing and even more resources neglect.

The ancient icebreaker *Healey*'s struggles in recent years was clear evidence of just that, being prematurely taken from its repair shipyard and catching fire once more before even reaching its Northwest Passage assigned patrol route.

So as politically contentious as the new Commandant's decision had been it was up to the Coast Guard's many supporters to accommodate the reality of these cuts by stepping up wherever and whenever possible. It was the type of open public/private communication that would be needed now more than ever, as the Coast Guard would <u>have to</u> return continued positive results with even fewer of their own personnel.

Snake assured her that the staff of Cape and Cliff Safety, Inc. would always be at the ready when research, equipment assessment, community liaison, S, H, or E help, or missions needed a private sector friend.

One such example was a new type of equipment that CSI had already provided to several major shipping clients for their preliminary evaluations. It was equipment that the Coast Guard had not even had an opportunity to fully study themselves, yet.

The equipment was a forward facing television monitor with night time infra-red capability, called, **SEA.AI**. It alerts crews early and reliably about nearly any objects on the surface of the water.

Using latest camera technologies in combination with artificial intelligence, **SEI.AI** detects and classifies objects, including those that escape conventional detection systems like radar or AIS.

Objects like:
- floating drug bales,
- un-signal equipped watercraft,
- floating obstacles like containers,
- adrift buoys,
- inflatable emergency rafts,
- kayaks,
- and persons overboard.

Commandant Fagan was certainly interested in the early results of this equipment's deployment in American vessels at sea and Snake assured her that she would be kept informed.

Chapter 12

Back in the headlines was the force for evil, the Malta-flagged, but Russia controlled, *MV Ruby*. Weeks earlier she had grounded twice suffering rudder and hull damage while carrying a full load of the explosion enhancing fertilizer ingredient ammonium nitrate, on behalf of mother Russia.

Since that time numerous countries and ports had barred the *Ruby* from docking resulting in her recent wandering existence.

Some reports initially referred to the bulk carrier being Russian-owned, but it is owned by a Maltese firm and sails under the island nation's flag.

Bouncing from closed port to closed port for weeks, Malta herself had even prohibited her to dock.

Having undergone temporary repairs in Tromso in Norway, she was cleared to return to sea by surveyors and the Maltese authorities on September 5, 2024, to find a port for permanent repairs while being under escort by tugs throughout the voyage.

But no ports have been willing to grant her passage into their harbors.

For over three weeks, the vessel was anchored in the southeast coast of the United Kingdom, in the English Channel, off the coastline of the county of Essex, an unsettling circumstance for the English people while the world looked for an accommodating port to effectively off-load this dangerous cargo then complete necessary repairs.

Finally in very late October 2024 the *MV Ruby* was given permission to dock at the Port of Great Yarmouth it was confirmed.

Its 20,000 tons of ammonium nitrate would be taken out of the ship—more than seven times the amount involved in the devastating

2020 Beirut blast—and damage to its hull and propeller would be repaired.

"The Port of Great Yarmouth will safely welcome the *MV Ruby*, in order to fulfill our obligations as Statutory Harbour Authority and assist the vessel with transshipment of its cargo," said Richard Goffin, Port Director for the Port of Great Yarmouth. "The Port of Great Yarmouth has the capability to handle hazardous materials and the discharge and transshipment of such materials and cargo is common practice across our port group."

Goffin further assured, "Our team is well-versed in implementing rigorous safety protocols and we strictly adhere to all UK safety regulations and international maritime standards.

The decision to allow the *MV Ruby* into UK waters has been approved by the UK Government and The Department for Transport."

Sir Roger Gale, MP for Herne Bay and Sandwich, after meeting with Shipping Minister Mike Kane, stated that the cargo is safe. "I do not believe my constituents face any threat to their security as a result of the presence of this vessel eleven miles off the North Kent coast," he wrote on X.

The vessel was initially anchored in the European Economic Zone but moved closer to shore due to inclement weather in the North Sea. While the damage has not rendered the ship unseaworthy, it requires repairs, which can only be carried out after the cargo is unloaded.

"We take our responsibilities as Statutory Harbour Authority[26] incredibly seriously and work closely with the relevant regulatory bodies to maintain full compliance.

Our role is to ensure that the *MV Ruby* is able to safely discharge and continue with its onward journey," added Goffin.

Chapter 13

Cape Safety, Inc. had a very impressive contact list that included

- world leaders,
- celebrities,
- CEO's of wide ranging industries,
- academicians,
- labor leaders of every industry
- futurists and theoretical planners
- architects
- maritime professionals
- military experts
- legal professionals
- medical experts in the vanguard of their specialties
- naturally, fellow safety, health and environmental professionals,
- transportation planners
- space exploration technologists
- undersea professionals

and so many more.

CSI's staff members were routinely in touch with most of them and they in turn routinely contacted CSI for some type of help.

These were not phone numbers, rarely if ever called, put into some database for prestige alone. No these were faces the staff knew usually on a first name basis, were considered friends as well as colleagues, and were people who the staff relied on as partners in knowledge.

The relationships were positive as well as productive and essential for the wellness of the planet.

This month Jeremy Tacklebox and Sue Mei had been the "lucky ones" picked to arrange the monthly meeting that typically brought as many consultants together as possible for a company update and an educational session.

Oh yes. Five star food was often served as well.

When it came to staging these meetings there was also an element of one-upping your coworkers that couldn't be denied. Favors were often called in to make the night a success and typically the cooperation was gratefully extended for prior CSI favors in their direction.

This month Sue would be tugging on a couple of strings. But creativity came easy to her and maybe there was a reason for that.[27]

The location she picked was a break room topic of PBS TV show discussion for the past several years, but a spot no one had yet visited.

So Sue decided that An **Escape to the Chateau** might be just the thing.

The owners of the Chateau, Richard Strawbridge and his wife Angel, had chronicled their reconstruction efforts for years on the show and had brought the Chateau from a Wicked Witch of the West castle to a Snow White Castle week after week right in front of viewers' eyes. CSI consultants had marveled at their castle transformation.

It was a miracle "home improvement" in no small part due to Dick Strawbridge's apparently endless abilities. The man is an engineer and demonstrates those skills daily.

Before Dick had singlehandedly installed a tube elevator requiring 1/8th inch clearances on three separate floor levels, Mike and Lars had known Dick for years, and were both well aware of his vast toolbox of skills.

The third of seven children, Dick was born in Burma, but raised and educated in Northern Ireland. He attended Ballyclare High School before going to Welbeck where he was Head of College. Dick then attended the Royal Military Academy Sandhurst, and in 1979, was commissioned into the Royal Corps of Signals.

In 1993 he was awarded an MBE for distinguished service in Northern Ireland, retiring as a Lieutenant Colonel in 2001 having served in Germany, England, the Caribbean, the Middle East and Northern Ireland.

After leaving the army, Dick had a successful career as a Program Manager, and then trouble shooter, for a large multinational company before becoming a full-time television presenter and author.

It was somewhere during that troubleshooter period that their paths had predictably crossed and each had helped the other across many countries, controversies, and crises.

Dick also had an honours degree in Electrical Engineering and received an additional Honorary Doctorate of Science from Plymouth University before "retiring" to convert a decrepit castle in France into a structure of international wonder serving as public vacation destination, banquet facility, and gourmet restaurant.

Sue had called for a reservation for a small group of 25 or so and Dick sounded delighted to accommodate. Naturally to get them all there to the French castle and back, within a reasonable time frame, would necessitate appropriate transportation.

It was another favor for Sue to call in.

Humans would soon be flying from the UK to the US at supersonic speeds, bragged a new airline company, started by another of those friends of CSI. The friend was CEO and founder Blake Scholl of Supersonic Boom, Inc.

His new design for the plane, called *Overture*, was revealed at Farnborough Air Show in the UK recently and had caught the eye of Sue.

During the plane's dedication Blake said in a speech, "Aviation has not seen a giant leap in decades. *Overture* is revolutionary in its design, and it will fundamentally change how we think about distance."

Sue wondered if a few consultants couldn't hitch a ride on the next intercontinental practice run that the article said they were now running routinely.

Nicknamed, 'Son of Concorde,' which used to hold the record for being the world's fastest commercial plane before it was retired in 2003, "With more than 600 routes across the globe, *Overture* will make the world dramatically more accessible for tens of millions of passengers," Blake had predicted.

Overture had been designed by Supersonic Boom, with four engines, designed to carry around 65-80 passengers at supersonic speeds of up to 1,305 miles per hour—twice as fast as current commercial planes.

The plane had also been developed to be more environmentally friendly, flying on 100 percent sustainable aviation fuel (SAF), and achieving net zero carbon emissions. Essentially, running on what could be cooking oil.

The plane would start being made in 2024, but would not carry its first proper passengers until around 2029/2030. But these improper Cape Cod passengers would gladly stow away aboard the prototype to get to the old continent that much quicker.

When this plane eventually comes on line for business it will become the world's fastest commercial plane with the potential to travel from New York in the US to London in the UK in three and a half hours, instead of six and a half!

And their preferred guest speaker, to be sure, would be with them as well—Daniel Levitin. Daniel was hoping to share with the staff some success stories with music therapy that had already been put in place.

Refugees and asylum seekers, it was well documented, faced extremely dangerous traumatic experiences in their home countries, and many of them faced dangerous escapes from them.

Leaving homes results in multiple losses—identity, culture, family, support networks and more; and results in severe psychological effects such as post traumatic stress disorder (PTSD), emotional disorders, anxiety and general grief.

Music is one thing that can remind displaced persons of home and family and their former life and is the one thing they can take with them.

In New South Wales, the Service for the Treatment and Rehabilitation of Torture and Trauma Survivors (STARTTS) offers music therapy to Mandaen and Assyrian communities, like popular and traditional music from Iraq. This empowers them to again use their individual voices and deepens the sense of cultural identity. Singing also, it has been proven, has physical, social, and emotional benefits. Singing releases endorphin reducing feelings of depression and anxiety, making people feel uplifted. The action of singing strengthens the lungs, improves posture, and increases oxygen flow to the bloodstream and brain. Singing slow and soothing tunes facilitates relaxation, slowing down respiration and heart rates. Singing in a group is also an icebreaker to people overwhelmed with shyness and nervousness. Being the "conductor" for the group reinforces their capacity to lead.

Luxembourg's Music Therapy Association implemented a program for underage asylum seekers encouraging them to play noisy instruments to blow off steam alternating with calming soft instruments for relaxation.

It, too, has demonstrated success.

Daniel also planned to tell the group how extracting key features from music and matching them to an individual's preferences, needs, or conditions will usher in a new age of music therapy that can augment and maybe displace the medicinal solutions used presently.

Music therapy personalized is already showing this kind of promise. Music therapies targeted at specific brain areas are scientifically proving to provide pain relief in clinical studies. In some well targeted instances even releasing the pain sensations.

It was the type of effort that required support from people like the consultants of CSI, who were open to alternative approaches and would expose clients, friends, associates, and their media contacts to new interventions to move the world forward.

Sue and Jeremy felt pretty comfortable that the meeting would be a hit and that they had set a high bar for the next "lucky ones" to exceed.

Chapter 14

Cape Safety, Inc. began as a humble safety and health shop visiting New England manufacturing plants, construction sites, and other workplaces to assist their safety, health and environmental concerns.

The provided assistance that would allow such enterprises to grow economically, employ even more workers, and simultaneously build a safe and thriving organization.

In the early 2020's CSI in Cape Cod had build such a reputation for excellence that for geographic and travel reasons alone, they needed a west coast presence as well, and Cliff Safety, Inc. was built-out and started.

Their dedication to those causes and companies had never wavered and providing assistance to American enterprises was still their core mission.

Paraphrasing the ironic adage, "If you want something done fast give it to a busy company,"[28] the firm's many accomplishment begat many, many, side roads for other noble, albeit often profitable as well, purposes.

But without building the two entities into Arthur D. Little or IBM sized international management think tank companies, Mike and Lars needed to refer more and more efforts to firms of that scope who would tackle the issue with the same verve as CSI always did. It was difficult balance since the bigger that type of consulting firm got, the more institutional they always became, more corporate they always became, more conservative they always became, and less reluctant to grab a political tiger by the tail they always became.

So when a present client, or potential client, had a thorny issue with political potential, Lars and Mike, routinely would keep that intervention even when one of those "ask Marcum" or "get BDO" companies, all well-known to CSI, had more immediate manpower for it.

CSI had many connections but never wanted one of those to color their approach to some client problem. When a decision was in the best S, H, or E interest of the client, they never wanted to look away from it because some conflict with another organization, political position, friendship, or country, was casting a shadow.

Mike had, at times, applauded the biggest entities out there and only days later had also jumped ugly on the same entities for their transgressions. He always wanted that freedom for all of his staff.

The United States Government was among those entities as were Amazon, Microsoft, Maersk, among others.

Pete Buttigeig, Secretary of Transportation, presently, who Mike quietly hoped would also become President one day, fell into that both friend and foe category of CSI's punching bag one day then hero the next.

Today one of those oddball issues was brought to his attention. It was off their typical track and involved a big giant (once again).

Over the past few years CSI's missions had morphed, by design and client request both, away from just the human condition and toward animal justice and overall earth science justice.

As it has become more apparent that we are a small and far more interdependent planet than we once saw ourselves, these causes had been recognized by CSI as equally essential.

Whale extinction, octopus farming, orca captivity, lobster and crab die-offs, rain forest elimination, carbon capture, fossil fuel depletion, nuclear blast power forest fires occurring and increasing drought severity—all had become matters as critical to man's survival as more obvious issues of worker health maintenance.

Safety wasn't just identifying rickety ladders any longer.

So the line for CSI had become admittedly blurred, and more and more they were judgment calls.

This issue fell somewhere on that spectrum.

5.9 million donkeys were being killed every year to produce a special kind of gelatin used in "youth-preserving" cosmetic products and supplements that claim to both enhance health and preserve youth. And the demand was growing.

Some donkeys were being skinned alive. Those that die being transported are often skinned on the spot, with their remains discarded by the side of the road. If they survived the journey, the donkeys are bludgeoned to death on arrival.

Many of these animals represented the way many in poor rural communities made a living by selling donkey transported water in jerry cans to remote customers. These animals were now being stolen and slaughtered by poachers in places like Nairobi and many other parts of Africa.

Ironically, the skin care product was in highest use by wealthy Chinese women, but without donkeys the poorer women of this same country and Africa would, once again, be the ones to do the heavy carrying the donkeys had done. A women against women calamity.

It seemed to CSI that they could help stop this cruelty and unconscionable deprivation of income to so many.

eBay had already banned the sale of "**ejiao**" gelatin and it seemed time that for retail giant **Amazon** to follow suit and stop participating in the murder of these intelligent creatures.

Donkeys are affectionate animals with incredible memories. They are an integral part of some communities in Africa and Asia that rely on them for transporting goods and people.

This helps free many women and girls in rural areas from hard physical labor and domestic chores.

But now donkeys were being slaughtered to meet the global demand for donkey skins containing **Ejiao**, whatever the hell that was.

Companies like CSI were being asked to advocate to Amazon that people from all around the world are calling on them to protect donkeys from inhumane treatment.

Last year a legal settlement forced Amazon to stop selling donkey gelatin in California.

California has been often ridiculed for leading the charge for Progressive improvements in America, and this same boldness had been one of the key reasons the firm expanded there. Amazing how, years later, the nation routinely caught up to "crazy" California and passed similar initiatives for their own states and sometimes the interests of other international concerns.

Now it was time for the movement to protect donkeys everywhere and roll out the ban against destroying them for a nebulous cosmetics use worldwide.

CAPE SAFETY, INC. - EVENTS WON'T STOP   101

Amazon ran a good national fleet, were making driver training improvements all the time, and were employing a lot of Americans, all good things.

But they were not treating warehouse workers well, and were not responsive to Mike's arguments to them about their politically insensitive algorithms that literally were "recommending other products you may like" such as the additional chemicals needed to complete an order for successful suicide cocktails, when only one of the chemicals had been requested. That was unconscionable. The bigger picture of Amazon's collective damage to America's downtowns was clearly evident, too, but that argument went beyond CSI.

Mike would put out a statement to their worldwide network to throw some more light on the need for this **Ejiao** ban. It would help, he had no doubt.

But it was the type of issue that more and more was pulling on the precious time and resources that were Cape and Cliff.

Chapter 15

What Mike and Lars had for the corporation's assets amounted to a sneeze in a hurricane but the principle of it was what mattered.

After over a year of urging Israeli restraint following the cowardly and wholly unjustified October 7, 2023, massacre of 1,200 young concertgoers in Israel, Mike felt that Washington and the corporate powers in this country were completely dismissive to that call for peace.

Israel's subsequent occupation of Palestinian land is illegal, the International Court of Justice has confirmed, and their destruction of Gaza in the name of peace was a mockery.

The Advisory Opinion of the UN's highest court made clear that helping to maintain the occupation was illegal, too.

But that's exactly what CSI's banks and pension funds were doing when they continued to help finance Israel's arms supplies. Even with lavish government support, Western arms manufacturers couldn't last a day without help from financial institutions. And some financiers were seriously considering their options. Mike felt that maybe a letter could help in their decision-making.

Norway's biggest private pension fund cut ties to Caterpillar for its role with Israel's army, even before the court's opinion was announced.

It was time that they all took action to cut Netanyahu's weapons supply and stop aiding and abetting Israel's illegal occupation. Banks, insurers and pension funds all needed to stop doing business with companies supplying arms to Israel. Arms were not the way to reconciliation with the Palestinian population.

In Europe alone, 20 banks had already provided 36.1 billion Euros in loans and underwritings to Israel's biggest international arms suppliers in 2019-2023.

A study published in June identified France's BNP Paribas as the biggest lender to Israel's top arms suppliers (4.7 billion Euros), followed by Crédit Agricole, Deutsche Bank, and Barclays Pension funds and insurers are also named in the NGO report and by UN experts who warned that if they fail to respond now, financial institutions linked to Israel's arms suppliers risk becoming complicit in war crimes.

Big US and Canadian banks were just as complicit. New York's Citigroup, for example, led a consortium of banks that helped the Israeli government buy its F35 jets. The bank has also invested billions more in Israel's arms suppliers since October 2023.

"But they can also divest, and help end this horror," so wrote Mike on behalf of CSI.

Some may say that governments should decide this sort of thing, and bankers should just stick to their jobs and make money. Indeed, our politicians have a lot to answer for, and some of them may end up behind bars some day for their part. But bankers are people too, and with enough public pressure, they can be moved to use their power for good.

So Mike was telling his bankers: don't do business with companies supplying arms to Israel.

More than 1,000 Palestinian children underwent leg amputations between October and November 2023 alone, according to UNICEF.

The numbers today would be even higher, except for the irony that Israeli bombs had decimated what was left of the Gaza hospitals doing those surgeries and the access roads to these same hospitals.

It looked to Mike like the nightmare would never end, and cutting Israel's arms supplies would take forever.

But as Nelson Mandela said, "It always seems impossible until it's done."

So for whatever it was worth, bringing more pressure to bear on the banks, insurers, and pension funds today deserved at least this letter of protest.

Whatever it might take to stop the bombings, thought Mike.

Oarlocks the cat strolled into Mike's office like it was his own, pounced on Mike's lap and demanded attention. Immediately if not sooner, since he had mice to chase and cat snacks to be eaten.

As he was stroking the tri-color attention strumpet cat, Lars walked in as well and gave out a hearty laugh at the profile of Mike behind his desk, stroking a cat in a manner very reminiscent of a Hollywood movie.

"Well if it isn't Dr. Evil," said Snake.

"Yes, and whatever your problem is we can solve it with some sharks with laser beams attached to their heads," Mike countered.

For the moment they both laughed. Then Snake got serious. It went that way a lot around both buildings. Without the gags the bad news they always dealt with could get overwhelming. So they needed the moments of brevity.

"We've been dealing with this problem for years and it just won't go away," said Snake.

"What's the saying, something about a bad penny?"

"It's that God-Damned cattleship business again.

Sam Plimsoll wanted it banned when he wrote his book about it back in 1890[29]. We all should have listened to him then and done it."

Snake was just made aware that secret cameras had captured disturbing visuals of Irish bull calves being tortured at a cattle export facility in Kerry.

The footage, which was recorded in March at Hallissey Livestock Exports near Killarney, showed calves being hit in the face, dragged by their ears and tails, and force-fed.

It was shared as part of an *RTÉ Investigates* report that aired on Prime Time.

Animal welfare expert Dr Simon Doherty of Queen's University Belfast described the calves' treatment as cruel.

He said that footage of calves being kicked, slapped, and stabbed with tools was and is inappropriate. Doherty believed that the handling of animals should be gentle and supportive rather than aggressive. It was CSI's philosophy as well. Cattleships and their holding pens could be humanly run. It just cost a slight amount more in money and worker energy.

The footage also showed dead calves being left in a pile outside in the rain, raising serious concerns about transmission of diseases.

"Absolutely unacceptable," uttered Snake.

Dr. Doherty stated that some of the calves seemed to have been dead for weeks, with their bodies decaying in the open air. He warned that this could risk the health of other animals, even people, nearby.

The investigation followed a similar one conducted in July 2023, which exposed the mistreatment of Irish calves during live export. After the incident, then-Taoiseach Leo Varadkar criticized the conduct as "repugnant" and demanded a thorough inquiry.

Denis Drennan, president of the Irish Creamery Milk Suppliers Association (ICMSA), saw the new footage and expressed his disappointment. He said that scenes of calves being beaten with sticks and made to travel while unfit are completely illegal and unacceptable.

The footage showed two calves being force-fed with stomach tubes. Drennan questioned why such sick calves were in the facility at all, saying they should never have been allowed to travel. He said that it is clearly mentioned in the regulations that animals unfit for travel should not be moved.

Hallissey Livestock Exports reacted to the footage through a solicitor, saying that they provide a valuable service to farmers and always try to adhere to animal welfare standards. They also stated that the Department of Agriculture regulates their company.

Despite these claims, the footage has raised new concerns about how Irish calves are treated before being exported. Per Ethical Farming Ireland, over 183,000 calves under six weeks old were exported from Ireland to Europe in 2023.[30]

So many of these ill treatments of animal issues had foreseeable human ramifications.

If not a direct disease potential, maybe a blow to the yet-to-be-well explored man/animal interface, and at the very least this indecent animal treatment was an affront to humanity's better angels.

This wasn't the first time CSI had cattleship issues and it probably wouldn't be the last. But Covid had taught the CSI consultants that the separation between animal and human health was a more porous barricade than we all had ever realized before 2020.

Chapter 16

Three of the Cliff Safety, Inc. gang today were hanging in the break room, the former Cliff House Restaurant, looking at a funny **Cartertoon** from the pen and mind of Jon Carter, and laughing. How could you not?

The laughter was, however, interrupted by their personal holograms providing them with their daily updates.

Sue Mei's hologram today was Tim Walz, Minnesota Governor and Vice Presidential candidate; Liza's was Oprah, and Alice's was Beyoncé.

So visually the ghostlike images of Tim, Oprah, and Beyoncé were all chattering in different corners of the room to their respective consultants about similar company information and headlines. All the holograms were leading with the California news that lawmakers had just passed a bill that would ban octopus farming and the sale of farmed octopus meat. A good news story to kick off their reports.

Octopuses are highly intelligent, complex creatures with unique personalities that even play together. Unfortunate for them we have classified them with other non-backboned creatures like slugs, snails, and clams. Hell, clams don't even have brains.

Yet one Spanish seafood giant in particular was racing to open the first ever octopus mega-farm, where one million of these unique animals would be stuffed into crowded tanks, then inevitably subjected to slow, stressful deaths.

CAPE SAFETY, INC. - EVENTS WON'T STOP

The three were hopeful that once again, as went California, so too went the rest of the nation's states, and then the rest of the world.

To meet the growing demand for octopus meat (and even that demand was being encouraged by big marketing efforts not any culinary consciousness of a marvelous new food), corporations had been racing to find ways to breed octopus in captivity.

The seafood mega-giant Nueva Pescanova was planning on building a one million large captive octopus farm in the Canary Islands.

It needed to be discouraged.

Captive octopuses often manage to escape, and when they can't they've been known to eat their own arms in their escape efforts and die in distress.

A worldwide lobbying effort was needed to discourage the Madrid conglomerate.

If the people of the world knew more about these fabulous animals the good people of California felt confident that they, too, would agree to ban this sea life captivity.

The Orca's in SeaWorld were demonstrating that man had no right to kidnap thinking species for any of man's selfish "reasons."

Massive factory farms on land for creatures like cows and pigs were known to be a mistake now as well, both to our health and to our environment. CSI had dealt extensively with those employers in times past.[31]

Replicating the mistake off of the world's coasts was simply irresponsible. Fellow west coast state Washington had already done the same, so California was not alone this time.

To anyone fortunate enough to have watched the Netflix Original documentary film directed by Pippa Ehrlich and James Reed, titled, *My Octopus Teacher*, it is more than apparent that these creatures possess intelligence, human recognition, personalities, and sensitivities not heretofore associated with ocean life. These are all characteristics deserving more respect from man than to be farmed and eaten.

The movie documents a year spent by filmmaker Craig Foster forging a relationship with a wild common octopus in a South African kelp forest. At the 93rd Academy Awards, it won the award for Best Documentary Feature.

Octopuses are solitary animals that need to move freely. Living in captivity in an extremely tight space with millions of other octopus is not species-appropriate and will lead to slow and agonizing deaths for them. Scientists and oceanographers have told us this in many forums[32]. We know this for fact now.

The people of Madrid were in the vanguard presently in this OCTO (Oppose Cruelty to Octopuses) movement and needed the world's, and CSI's, support.

CSI had many, probably most, of the world's aquariums as clients.

Most of them, Sue felt, would be persuadable to put pressure on this firm to reconsider. Major food buyers like the U.N. and José Andrés of World Central Kitchen would be supportive too.

There wasn't a new market for this particular seafood and this firm would need to talk that up should their project come to fruition. Why go to those marketing efforts to persuade people to eat the wrong thing when alternative foods were healthier and kinder? Plant based foods could use better marketing instead, for instance. The world's population needed to become more mindful of what they were consuming and why.

This soft-bodied, eight-limbed mollusk of the order Octopods, with so much more to "Teach" us, deserved a better future than becoming a fashionable new link in the human food chain.

Maybe capturing animals for non-food purposes was more justified.

But that needed full scrutiny, too.

The firm respected the argument that capturing animals in the wild and exhibiting them in aquariums under the care of scientists and others committed to their welfare was different. "They are ambassadors from the wild and unless people know about what these animals are all about they won't be interested in their stewardship," went that argument with some legitimacy. Sending such fish, mammals and sea creatures to accredited institutions where people can see them in a recreated natural habitat where they will live longer than in nature was an honest argument for the continuation of those facilities. Boston's aquarium was one of the first in the nation to offer naturalistic settings for all its animals. It was a visionary change, one that not only made its exhibits more educational for the public, but also made it far more interesting for its animal inmates. Under controlled conditions, visitors could even touch the octopuses and in kind the octopuses could attach their suction pads onto the aquarium visitor to mutually learn about each other. There was full evidence that the sea creatures through sight and touch recognized one person from another and knew why the guest was there, for feeding, cleaning or simply visiting.

But tiny tanks for giant orcas that had bore no resemblance to their ocean lives, and then *neglecting them until the next show was abusive. There was a clear difference.*

So Sue, a self identified autism spectrum member, house lawyer and S, H, and E consultant at CSI, went to work preparing appropriate messages for her two communications wizards, Alice and Liza, to turn into properly directed worldwide requests for intervention.

Chapter 17

While cohorts were working on west coast projects with many *tentacles*, Snake and Candace had made their ways, separately, to Colonel's Island Terminal, site of one of the nation's largest auto and roll-on/roll-off facilities, in Georgia.

The site would provide a realistic backdrop for industry, terminal and governmental participants to test their emergency response strategies. After a couple of recent serious RO/RO ship fire incidents in New Jersey and Georgia, where in one of the cases a ship sinking at the dock was narrowly avoided, this was a proactive effort to do better during any future incidents.

In a proactive response to the growing risks associated with electric vehicle (EV) transportation, the U.S. Coast Guard recently was spearheading a crucial multi-agency exercise focused on tackling vessel fires caused by electric vehicles' lithium-ion batteries.

The two-day drill will bring together an array of federal, regional, state, local, and industry partners to enhance coordination and preparedness for such emergencies. Hosted by the Coast Guard Marine Safety Unit Savannah, the exercise will be centering on validating the Coastal Georgia Area Contingency Plan (ACP) in line with the National Preparedness and Response Exercise Program (NPREP).

The scenario will simulate an EV fire aboard the American Roll-On Roll-Off Carrier (ARC) *Arc Integrity* while docked at Georgia Ports Authority's Colonel's Island Terminal.

Coast Guard Marine Safety Unit Savannah along with federal, regional, state, local agencies and industry partners conduct exercises to validate the Coastal Georgia Area Contingency Plan in Brunswick, GA, from Sept. 24-25, 2024. The incident scenario focused on a simulated electric vehicle fire onboard the *ARC Integrity*. (Courtesy Photo)

The exercise comes after several recent high-profile vessel fires[1] where electric vehicles were involved including the Simons Island wreck *Golden Ray*.

"People and partnerships are vitally important to the resiliency of the marine transportation system. Exercises such as these help first responders understand their various roles and responsibilities throughout complex emergencies within the maritime environment and foster unity of effort, collaboration, and coordination," said Cmdr.

---

1. https://gcaptain.com/a-brief-look-back-at-recent-car-carrier-fires/

Nathaniel Robinson, commanding officer of Marine Safety Unit Savannah and Captain of the Port, talking with Candace.

The exercise, which took over seven months to plan, involves collaboration from several federal, state, and local agencies, as well as key industry players like ARC, Gallagher Marine Systems, and Georgia Ports Authority (GPA).

The preparation underscores the seriousness with which authorities are approaching the potential hazards of lithium-ion battery fires[2] on vessels.

In the lead-up to the exercise, ARC demonstrated its commitment to safety by providing familiarization tours of their vessels to more than 100 local firefighters at the Port of Brunswick, further bolstering regional preparedness.

The timing of this exercise is particularly pertinent, coming on the heels of back-to-back hurricanes Helene and Milton hitting the U.S. Southeast.

The U.S. Coast Guard has previously issued warnings[3] about the extreme risks associated with loading damaged EVs onto commercial vessels.

It was an issue CSI had been out in front on for years. CSI had also been a leading advocate of new fire detection and suppression technologies in recent months on behalf of several shipping clients. Salt water's effects on poorly sealed batteries had also been a CSI in-house topic of discussion in the recent past, so both Candace and Snake already had considerable intellectual and shoe leather skin in the game of shipboard lithium fire events.

Marine Safety Alert 01-23[4], issued in 2023, directly addresses this issue and provided critical recommendations for the maritime industry

---

2. https://gcaptain.com/tag/battery-fire/

3. https://gcaptain.com/u-s-coast-guard-says-to-avoid-loading-electric-vehicles-with-saltwater-damage-on-ships/

following Hurricane Ian, where saltwater exposure led to numerous EV fires.

"Vessels, ports, and shippers should be aware of this extreme risk and avoid loading EVs with damaged Lithium-Ion onto commercial vessels," the safety alert stated.

As the global demand for electric vehicles continues to rise, so does the potential for lithium-ion battery fires at sea. Through simulating real-world scenarios and validating response equipment and firefighting capabilities, the Coast Guard and its partners were hoping to establish a new benchmark in maritime safety preparedness, allowing them to adapt to the emerging challenges posed by the transportation of electric vehicles and their potent lithium-ion batteries.

Freemantle Highway Ro/Ro fire at sea[33]

The hulk of the *Freemantle Highway* is loaded onto a heavy lift ship for transport to a repair shipyard in October 2024

---

4. https://www.dco.uscg.mil/Portals/9/DCO%20Documents/5p/CG-5PC/INV/Alerts/USCGSA_0123.pdf?ver=dsWGAVKadU3cr4CJZZAUYw%3d%3d

Manufacturing in Massachusetts, once the firm's bread and butter customers, had certainly fallen as a percentage of CSI's income in the past two decades. It now barely showed on their balance sheet.

But those workers had not been forgotten by the folks at Cape Safety, Inc.

Although many, dare we say most, major worker safety hazards had been addressed through an involvement with CSI or simply by following the recommendations of insurance safety engineers or OSHA voluntary compliance officers, danger never took a day off.

So it was with a bit of nostalgia, but a bit of vigilance also that William was reading a *Boston Globe* article[34] writing about what was still being made in Massachusetts. It was enlightening.

In Fall River, **Vanson Leathers** was still cutting and stitching leather jackets, gloves and pants. One of their sewing machines was made when Roosevelt was President. *Theodore Roosevelt.*

William had heard the stories from Bob Guard, the long retired founder of CSI, talking about his visits to such plants in the 1970's when they were still being powered by overhead line shafting and leather connecting belts; when the stinky hides were hand run through tight rollers to squeeze out the nasty juices; when cookie-cutter dies were used with beam dinker machines to maximize hide utilization; and when every other employee would greet you with a four- sometimes a three-finger handshake because the equipment had caught them at some point during an inattentive moment.

In Norwell, the premier cymbal maker for orchestras, rock bands, and every type of music in between, **Zildjian,** was still going strong. The company, originating in Turkey, had its share of occupational health concerns with the melting of metals to make over 500 different models of cymbals. Gene Wing, Bob's partner and original Industrial Hygienist, had taken many an air sample in that plant and assisted them with ventilation upgrades and the selection of proper personal protective equipment.

Verne Q. Powell, in Maynard, MA, and **Burkhart Flutes**[35] **and Piccolos** in Shirley, MA, were manufacturers of musical woodwinds. Their customers have included Eric Dolphy in the band of Charlie Mingus and John Coltrane; Ian Anderson of Jethro Tull; and William Kincaid considered to be "the father of the American flute school." Verne Powell, born in 1879, started the company by melting down a handful of silver half-dollars, 7 spoons and 3 watch cases to make his first "spoon flute." Any melting of metals brought safety risks like severe burns; health risks like respiratory impairment and musculoskeletal damage from lifting heavy metals.

All of these firms survived in high end markets now with few regional suppliers left to help them and with cheap foreign competitors always under-pricing their products.

Other Massachusetts firms mentioned were **Randolph Engineering**, maker of aviator style sunglasses to the military for over four decades. **Junior Mints** being made in a former Tootsie Roll factory in Cambridge. It was the only surviving candy maker among 66 former candy manufacturers in the same area.

The Acushnet Company was still making golf balls in two New Bedford Industrial Park located plants. No, the yelling of, "Fore,[36]" was not considered by CSI to be an acceptable risk management strategy to avoid safety and health hazards at those two plants.

John Matouk & Co. still produced Town and Country quality linens for those with an appetite to spend, say, $549 for a single flat queen sheet. Fortunately there were many of those folks out there.

Boston Boat Works in Charlestown was still launching about a dozen luxury carbon fiber boats a year and **Cape Cod Ship Building** in Wareham still kicked out new customized sailboats.

GE Aerospace in Lynn was still cranking out jet engines for the U.S. military, and the best friend peanut butter ever had, the **Marshmallow Fluff** plant was still producing the sticky white stuff here in the Bay State.

So too, **Polar Beverages** was still making oceans of beverages in Worcester. William understood that CSI had their factory and warehouse as a client for years and had even trained all their fleet drivers when the "then" new Commercial Driving License was established; **David Clark Company** made airplane and industrial use headsets; **Alden Shoes** and **New Balance Shoes** were holding on in an industry once owned by New England; **Amazon Robotics** and, of course, **Gillette**, the facial razor folks, ended their short list.

Many of the companies had history with **Cape Safety, Inc.** and in time if they continued to prosper, probably all would.

Chapter 18

The two Communication Centers kept buzzing with news and information for the staff to follow. Some of the news they'd need to respond to immediately, some would be prioritized for future action, and some would just need to be resolved without professional help.

It was why the firm couldn't separate their policies from the politics of the time.

One party wanted Democracy, the other wanted Fascism.

CSI would obviously have no role to play in a country no longer committed to social improvement and simply waiting for some end-of-times ultimate solution to all of mankind's problems.

They had no choice of who to support.

To them, some of the daily headlines had obvious solutions. But others were more complex requiring compromise and maybe even some sacrifice.

This whale news was an example of just that.

And for now put aside the SeaWorld Orca captivity issue which was a topic so complex that Lars and Claus had put it onto a future meeting agenda with several WHOI experts.

But this news was to the plight of the free Atlantic and Pacific whales, those that whale watching boats in Maine, Cape Cod, San Francisco, San Diego, Orange County, and Boston took visitors to meet every day.

"A record lobster seizure" of 13,000 pounds of lobster had just been made at a Nova Scotia processing facility in Canada. This $100,000 seizure represented more than one person committed to exploiting our oceans, although only one person had, so far, been arrested. First Nation fishermen were the whistle blowers on what had to have been an organized poaching effort maybe even international in scope with some United States lobstermen involved. Who and how would this black market lobstering be brought to justice and ended?

What more can the inshore fishing associations involved in this whistle blowing do, and should they be allowed to capture poachers' gear and patrol the waters themselves for out-of-season fishing infractions? Good questions in need of good answers.

Yet what about the continued deployment of even legal lobster gear?

Here in Massachusetts the first regional whale death of a young female North Atlantic Right Whale found with fishing gear wrapped around its tail had just added clear evidence to what whale advocates had been cautioning the fishing community for years.

The Maine lobster community had been resisting "rope-less traps" for years now despite warnings that traditional traps would inevitably lead to such a whale death.

Now it had happened and maybe NOAA finally needed to lower the boom. But Canada needed to do the same. Fishing gear is one of two primary death traps threatening the survival of these whales. Entangled animals either drown quickly or suffer agonizing injuries that eventually lead to starvation, infections, and slow, painful deaths of these mammals. The other death trap, inadvertent ship strikes, was already being addressed with mandated slow speeding, designated and drone patrolled shipping lanes, and required Coast Guard permissions for ship travel.

Forward thinking Maine lobstermen have been practicing with "rope-less" tackle for many months now and know how the gear works. Yes, it is more expensive and yes, setting traps will take longer, whether in Canadian or Maine waters, the point of dispute.

But these "critically endangered"[37] gentle giants need our help with only an estimated 360 left and fewer than 70 reproductive females.

The west coast Dungeness crab fishery in California was being asked for the same concession to reduce whale entanglements off of the Pacific coast. The Dungeness Crab Gear Working Group has been tirelessly testing this gear in recent seasons and has even considered grappling for deployed gear as another alternative to these self-raising traps. Experimental Fishing Permits (EFP's) approved by the California Fish and Game Commission approved the deployment of 23,048 rope-less traps with fishermen acknowledging a "learning curve" but truly finding no reason this alternative crabbing was unacceptable. 19 fishermen landed 229,000 lbs. of crab with an estimated landing value of $1.6 million, anything but a fishing failure.

And that was but one complex issue.

What about Cliff Safety, Inc. being asked for their opinion on the future of transportation in American cities?

The Luddites[38] in the discussion had apparently already raised the discussion to an argument.

Los Angelinos had recently grabbed a headline or two for hurling e-scooters into the ocean.

Residents of San Francisco and Chandler, Arizona, had been accused of sabotaging driverless cars.

Barcelonians recently squirted cruise ship passengers and shoppers with water in their form of protest against transportation in use to bring more people into their communities.

- Scooters were reportedly a symbol of *gentrification.*
- Driverless cars because they represented an *erosion in public trust.*
- Cruise ship passengers because they *symbolized, over-tourism.*

Were they noble protests against legitimate anti-city initiatives or stunts that only hurt the four cities' images as worthwhile visitation destinations?

Most importantly, how should cities respond to these ad-hoc protests?

- Do they ban scooters and other forms of fossil free

transportation as alternatives to gas guzzling taxis, Ubers, and Lifts?
- Are efforts to encourage city bicycles—both standard and powered—motorized skateboards, personal vehicles for the physically challenged, with special lanes and street schemes a bad idea?
- High speed rapid transit brings more people to cities. Should that be encouraged as a fossil fuel alternative or discouraged as a congestion cause?
- Do they restrict ships bringing tourists to their ports to fuel cell or renewable hydrogen powered cruise ships only? And would they necessarily carry fewer tourists if that is the primary issue?
- How about incoming planes? Should they have carbon fuel restrictions that, if so, would certainly reduce the size of planes landing at those airports?
- Do we begin to restrict city vehicle travel to essential vehicles only?
- Why not city visitations to essential visitors only?
- And is this visitor war a disguised political war between the "woke" tree-hugger mindset on the left vs. the "black fuel" Hummer drivers on the right?
- Or maybe the opposite with the, "I've got mine" <u>wealthy</u> city dwellers attempting to keep out any <u>too poor to afford city life</u> types?

City planners, architects, law enforcement, and those on the interface of modern transportation systems were somewhat flummoxed and were reaching out to specialists like CSI for answers (at least opinions).

Those in the know have noted that although cities tended to be enclaves of progressive politics, smaller cities leaning more conservative could escalate this by implementing restrictive or retaliatory policies like banning electric vehicles or the like.

One source[39] even postulated that "A dystopian version of this future produces a fractured transportation landscape in which whole fleets of commercial aircraft, cruise and cargo ships, autonomous vehicles, and other transportation modalities become welcome in some cities and unwelcome in others."

But maybe, like most transportation issues facing our country in times past they will be sorted out in the marketplace?

Living wages for Uber and Lyft drivers aren't being realized while the company owners are receiving record salaries and perks. How sustainable will that be?

Cities and ports that make visitors unwelcome, with squirt guns or other methods will quickly be taken off of cruise itineraries with the passengers' wallets emptying where they are more welcome.

Rental bikes and the like are in their earliest introductions and maybe are being seen as threats to existing systems. Tour guides who walk with groups supplanted by e-bikes and prerecorded tour scripts on headphones, jitney drivers losing customers to the novelty of powered skateboards, and the like. Such immediately affected workers are likely in the vanguard of Luddite-style damage to scooters, e-bikes, and other rental transportation equipment.

Devin felt that maybe these new players needed to think about offering more to the cities they plan to inhabit.

Maybe cruiseships could schedule to make their vessel available to that city's business community for conferences, or open their restaurant services to city citizens when they were in port?

Maybe autonomous vehicles could automatically provide (expensive for cities to maintain) urban lighting?

Maybe costly and underutilized night time municipal bus routes could be curtailed and replaced by an assist from autonomous vehicles?

And that was but a second complex issue.

It appeared that Cape Safety, Inc. was the place complex issues came to thrive.

Chapter 19

On the occasion of former President Jimmy Carter casting a vote in Georgia for Kamala Harris, just a few days following his 100th birthday, Heidi Holdgate, one of the soon to retire senior S, H, and E consultants at CSI, had been asked by Mike to "cook up a little presentation for the staff about this national grid situation."

A brief presentation on **"The Grid"** had been the topic of Gretchen Bakke's[40], over three hundred page book by the same name, and she "left lots of stuff out," so Heidi knew she had a tiger by the tail.

But Mike was aware of it, too, and rephrased the assignment as, "a dumbing down for us non-electrical engineers who still have a need to know."

Political legend will probably always have it that, politically, Ronald Reagan bested Jimmy Carter when entering the White House by removing White House rooftop solar panels Carter had installed. It couldn't be further from the truth. The panels were simply the shiny keys.

In the early days of commercial electricity, what we now call *the grid*, people didn't change their own light bulbs for fear of electrocution. Instead a trained bulb replacer was dispatched on a bicycle balancing a big sack of hand-blown vacuum-filled ampules on his back to replace all the bulbs that had burned out during the previous weeks.

We've come a long way.

In the early days and until recent decades the "power plants" were located alongside the source of the power. Not always wise but necessary. In 1956, the Niagara Falls generating station fell off the edge of the cliff at falls' edge, where it had been perched.

It was a total loss and one of the largest industrial accidents in America to that date.

Thirty-nine men escaped the plant as it fell. One worker was not so lucky and was "hurled through a window into the river" along with thousands of tons of debris.

But "power plants" fueled by coal, then natural gas, augmented by nuclear, have been the source of all electricity. Everything fed off of that reality including transmission, distribution, management, raw material supplies, and employment. Engineers and technicians wanting a grid career worked for and usually at power stations. Energy became pretty predictable, and redundant plants became interconnected so that higher energy demands could be pulled from other plants when needed; likewise plants could be taken off-line for maintenance without customer disruptions (even awareness); and during low demand plants could even be shut down.

Sure, there were multiple plants and players across the country all with their own personnel and networks so it would appear that there was no monopolistic practice.

Some governmental oversight of rates and such occurred but it was more *tail pretending it controlled the dog* than reality. Not dissimilar to how the NFL "organizes" over 30 separate enterprises called "teams," this system also maintained, charitably, general control of *the grid*.

But more than 70% of the grid's transmission lines and transformers are twenty-five years old; add nine years to that and you have the age of the average American power plant.

As a result significant power outages are climbing year by year, from 15 in 2001, to 78 in 2007, to 307 in 2011, the most of any developed nation.

By way of this news and update we return to President Jimmy Carter and a minor sub-clause of a sub-act of an omnibus bill to the National Energy Act.

The law, when passed, squeezed by Congress only by a single vote even during a national energy crisis when Americans were in gasoline rationing lines, being told by the President to wear a sweater, and were keeping their home heat turned down, all in the spirit of American patriotism.

But this little Jimmy Carter provision, thrown in at the last minute to give a helping hand to a wood chip co-generating company in tiny New Hampshire, and called the Public Utilities Regulatory Policies Act (PURPA), effectively, broke the utility consortium's control over everything that entered, moved through, and exited the grid.

Beyond the New Hampshire wood chip guy who worked out a deal with his local power plant immediately, nothing happened really for decades but the door was now open to thousands, maybe millions of Americans to become their own power plants and to participate in new power generation startups utilizing solar, wind turbines, hydro, water current, constant motion, and other energy sources. Moreover, the energy they couldn't use personally could be sold back to the grid at "market price" opening new doors to an unknown number of American entrepreneurs.

Ronald Reagan and his fossil fuel devotees and political sponsors never saw that tiny provision leading to so much new energy capacity that their massive power plants, in some places, would become at best the backup systems to the tremendous energy contributions of solar and wind farms now—and who knows what new power sources in the not so distant future.

Granted the new systems have issues, but so do the old and rapidly deteriorating existing utility plants. Nuclear waste remains an unsolvable problem. Just ask the folks in Plymouth, MA, where it all started, just up the road a piece from Cape Safety, Inc.

Authorities, assisted by the laboratories of Cape Safety, Inc. in Woods Hole, were still monitoring a nuclear cooling water settling pond there and remain unable to release it back to Cape Cod Bay due to public outrage. It has been nearly a decade since Plymouth Nuclear Power provided any energy to New Englanders.

The fossil fuel plants are steady night and day, windy or calm, but how long will their fossil fuels be available for us (some say no further than 2050) and what damage to the air we are breathing, with resulting climatic damage, will be suffered by everyone continuing to power our lives with power plants alone?

Millions of Americans were now employed in this effort resulting in the strongest economy on record.

New solar farms, everyplace. New wind turbines, everyplace. New battery manufacturing plants being built throughout the country. Infrastructure being planned to accommodate these new energy sources, record amounts of energy conservation by average people, small businesses, larger businesses, and monstrous skyscrapers under construction and development.

It was all apparent to anyone not in a political shame spiral being generated by selfish forces purely to keep one man from his long overdue justice. Any cult member claiming otherwise was knowingly gaslighting but even worse missing out at being a participant in this new wave of true energy independence from Middle East oil.

Those were some of the thoughts that Heidi was trying to get onto 3" by 5" note cards for her staff talk. No one ever said this job would be easy and she had been doing it now for, as she said, "a lotta years."

Chapter 20

Sandra Byrneski, had been CEO for more than a couple of years now and had managed to handle all that the job entailed plus she continued to run the Woods Hole laboratory as the Senior Industrial Hygienist.

William had managed to obtain an Industrial Hygiene (IH) Certification, too, with a few years of night school, and was probably poised to replicate Sandra's lab on the west coast if he could discipline his love life.

Mid-thirties, highly gregarious, a lover of history and the retelling of history, he had never had a problem getting company from a series of starlets when the firm first went west, then at least a couple of eastern beauties these days.

Although travel was constant for every consultant, Sandra's attempts at committing him to establish a home at Cliff Safety had, so far, not been answered affirmatively by William.

Sandra was hoping she could coerce him into a west coast commitment with the idea of his running his own lab there.

"So what do you think about taking command of that laboratory out there and cutting back on some of this insane travel? We could get you a lab tech or two and we could blow that part of our business out bigly?"

"I like the idea boss, I really do but I have this friend in Washington these days and we've been seeing each other every weekend."

"I understand, so what does she do?"

"Works for the CIA I think but naturally she doesn't tell me that. She goes into work through a dentist's office. Ostensibly she works there but she doesn't know a molar from a bowling ball, and it's a big old building that probably has all manner of back stairs and ways to get around. When she called one of my teeth a bicuspidore I was on to her."

"So does she travel everywhere like you?"

"No, I think she's stationed; assigned; located; whatever you'd call it, right there. She also knows way more about Russia and the Communist culture than any dental hygienist would ever need to know. She calls it her hobby but what single American woman picks up modern Russian history as a hobby?"

"Hate to bring it up my naïve employee, but has it ever dawned on you that she could be working for the other side?"

If anyone was there they'd kick themselves forever for not having a camera ready to catch the look on William's face when Sandra confronted him with the obvious.

"Jeezus, it never did until now," said William almost apologetically.

"Just be careful not to talk about any government clients we're working for in front of her, that's all, until you feel sure she's on our team. And don't leave out any paperwork on your desk."

"Yeah, absolutely. Now my guard is up. But that would explain how smooth this relationship has gone. Almost too perfect, do you know what I mean?"

Sandra was in her sixties and, age wise, William could have easily been her son, therefore, their talk that day was more in the general spirit of parental advice than a boss to employee warning.

"Hey, if it doesn't work out I can still use an answer on that relocation. It's not like you won't be back here two or three times a month, you know how that always goes. I'd just like to have an active backup lab as this one is starting to overwhelm me. Everybody wants something or other tested before they make a decision. Sometimes just because you can doesn't mean you should, get my drift? Some of these hurricane clients have green slippery slime floor to ceiling, the house looks like an algae swamp, and they want an industrial hygiene sampling before they leave.

People—it's bad—get the hell out of there. You don't need one of our reports to tell you that. Your eyes give you all the information you need!"

Both of them laughed at the vacillations of human nature and William assured Sandra that he wouldn't keep her hanging. He suddenly had some serious doubts about keeping this "hip" East Coast girl Washington connection going, and you know what the Beach Boys said about the always tanned "California girls."

Maybe players had to play—for at least a little while longer.

Sandra grabbed a Graham cracker to snack on and William couldn't refrain from making it another history teaching moment.

"You know who invented that?"

Naturally, she didn't.

"Sylvester Graham back in the 1830's[41]. He was a big healthy lifestyles advocate way back when no one even heard of such a health concept. Went to Amherst to continue a minister legacy in the family but was drummed out by other students. I read that he was a little too "woke" for college life even in the 1830's with a no-liquor and no-poorly-prepared foods lifestyle philosophy.

He and Ralph Waldo Emerson became big bran guys and their followers were called, 'Grahamites.'

So tip your hat to Sylvester for that snack. He was kicked out as a minister so one day you could have a Graham Cracker for an afternoon snack."

Sam interrupted Sandra's snack with news that a tragedy had just occurred in Mendenhall, Mississippi, as they were dismantling a bridge there.

Three employees of T. L. Wallace Construction were killed and four were injured Wednesday when the bridge collapsed over the Strong River in central Mississippi's Simpson County.

One of the injured workers was treated at the scene Wednesday and the other three remained hospitalized in critical condition.

The bridge was on state Route 149 and the road had been closed to traffic since as part of a bridge replacement project, the Mississippi Department of Transportation said. The Mississippi Department of

Transportation said one of its inspectors was at the work site when the bridge collapsed, and that person was unharmed.

U.S. Transportation Secretary Pete Buttigieg said that the Federal Highway Administration was "engaging state officials concerning" the "premature collapse during demolition of a bridge on State Route 149 in Mississippi."

"We must work to understand what caused this accident so we can prevent something like this from happening again," Republican Senator Cindy Hyde-Smith said.

Sandra rolled her eyes at the predictably lame verbal responses from both the Democratic Transportation Secretary and the Republican Senator who had never cast a vote of support for anything relating to construction worker safety.

"Megan, keep me posted on this, please," requested Sandra. "If we aren't getting more than thoughts and prayers for details, we'll think about sending someone down there. Demolition done right should never result in deaths and injuries. Something important went wrong that needs to be brought into the light soon. We have lots of demo projects happening nationwide and we must know what went wrong there. Those official investigation reports always take too long and stay too well hidden from the public."

Those drawn out governmental inquiries were a pet peeve that everyone at CSI shared. It was a problem getting worse all the time as the country grew more litigious at the expense of relaying necessary prevention information.

For instance it had been half a year since the implosion of the *Oceangate*[42] Inc. submersible submarine and only now had the Coast Guard assembled a team of witnesses to talk about it.

Thank goodness **Oceangate** didn't run a fleet of these Titan Submersibles at the time or surely there would have been a team of their lawyers begging to let more visits to the *Titanic* continue with identical vessels, while the *official report* was still being worked out.

David Lochridge, **Oceangate's** former Operations Director, had already testified that he felt let down by OSHA, who hadn't followed up on his complaints prior to the tragic dive of the *Titan*. So now, post-tragedy, it was the Coast Guard asking the questions. So many shortcuts had been taken by the mastermind of that company, Stockton Rush, that one witness had told the Coast Guard that Rush expected that this kind of end would inevitably protect Rush from ever having to face legal accountability for disregarding many, many, manufacturing safety protocols. Another engineer had testified that Rush could not handle criticism well and could not hear the word no.

Lochridge, predictably, had been fired by Rush for pointing out appalling defects in the submersible's design.

The innovative, but obviously inadequate, carbon fiber hull had delaminated and had previously cracked. It was a concern that had been glossed over by Rush who avoided subsequent integrity testing. Proof of the delaminating was placed in evidence.

Hull strain data irregularities that resulted in "a bang as loud as an explosion" occurred after the mini-sub's prior trip to a deep depth, and were also discussed.

This "bang noise" could have been layers in the carbon fiber parting or the hull separating from the titanium end rings.

"The degree of the separation can't be known, but it could have been the beginning of the end," so testified Phil Brooks, **Oceangate's** Director of Engineering.

Brook's request to return the sub at that point to company headquarters in Everett, Washington, to look for cracks was denied for financial reasons, and no further hull testing was ever conducted.

In this case a six-month Coast Guard delay to begin the "official report" made sense, since so no one else's lives were being likewise threatened in the interim.

But bridge demolition projects were happening everyplace with many construction workers' lives possibly involved.

If a common practice caused this tragedy, it needed to be outed right away. Not in six months' time.

The Marine Technological Society (MTS) Manned Undersea Vehicles (MUV) committee understood this and had been in the forefront of promoting safe and responsible deep ocean exploration for over 50 years and noted that until this event the industry had an admirable safety record through rigorous engineering practices, safety standards, and collaboration with federal agencies like the United States Coast Guard, United States Navy, and leading classification societies.

The third-party testing and validation protocols not followed by *Oceangate* were among those practices.

The 10 active vessels approved for depths of 4,000 meters or more and the 215 active vessels approved for lesser depth, serve diverse purposes, including personal use, but primarily for commercial ventures, submarine rescues, security operations, and to a far lesser extent tourism.

Following comprehensive operational standards is imperative during periods of rapid industry growth.

Sandra and CSI knew well that MTS continued to disseminate marine technology information, to promote educational efforts, and advance the development of tools for marine exploration of the oceans.

The World Submarine Organization's mission was to unite the global community, fostering innovation and safety through its annual symposium and advocacy for a universal submarine operations standard.

The WSO aimed to insure a legacy of safety and innovation, addressing jurisdictional issues and promoting global safety guidelines.

As the industry evolved, it was crucial to collaborate and prepare for future challenges.

These organizations[43] remained steadfast in their missions to advocate for responsible submersible operations, and safe ocean exploration.

Chapter 21

It seemed like maritime news when it first came in but it was really news about an inland project that Jeremy had been assisting at a few weeks earlier and was now ready once more for the public.

Cape Safety, Inc. had been asked to oversee revamped plans for a public landmark at the $25 billion, yes spelled with a b, Hudson Yards in New York, that had been violently misused, then shutdown, for reconsideration in 2021.

The Vessel, as it was called, provided a unique elevated walkway to tourists and locals at a ritzy development on the west side of Manhattan.

Tragically though, it had been misused in a string of suicides then shut down until a solution to that could be found.

Jeremy found just the solution through a closely coordinated effort with *The Vessel's* chief architect Thomas Heatherwick and Heatherwick Studio.

They had developed a floor to ceiling steel mesh on most levels that will be able to withstand the outdoor elements while preserving the unique experience of the spiral, zigzagging stairs, walkway architecture. The structure was the crown jewel of the gleaming midtown development and had already drawn millions of visitors from around the globe.

The new steel mesh will be designed to withstand any damage including from people trying to cut it. Four young people with various mental health concerns[44] had taken their lives from various levels of the 150-foot high sculpture and a prevention solution for the roof level still needed to be designed. This level would remain closed to visitors until that solution could be installed.

All involved desired the tragedies to be thought of as an issue in the past and never again. Hudson Yards and the families affected had, and continued to be, supportive of movements committed to that aim, particularly the ***SuicidePreventionLifeline.org.***

File that one under near miracles, Liza told Alice as they were both on the roof of Cliff Safety, looking out over the Pacific at a lot of containership traffic, while wiring up a new sophisticated antenna that would upgrade their satellite communications. Toughie, their rogue cat, had somehow also climbed the steep inside stairs leading to the roof and was warning seagulls that the roof was now his domain also.

Seagulls weren't buying it, but that was Toughie's problem.

Liza's news had just come in before they met on the roof so Alice hadn't heard the story from Dover, Delaware, that a police dispatcher there had just saved the life of a sailor in Dover, England.

"Seems that a man called the Dover Police Department when his brother phoned him that he was sinking in a boat somewhere in the English Channel," Liza said.

"But not the Dover, England, Police Department, but the Dover, Delaware, USA police department.

The dispatcher recognized that trying to refer the frantic caller to the authorities in England could cost valuable time, (Communications Operator MacKenzie Atkinson) so he kept the man on the line and began collecting critical information. The caller provided the coordinates of the vessel, and the operator, who had recently acquired certification from the International Academies of Emergency Dispatch, followed protocols for a vessel in distress," Liza told Alice.

Meanwhile the Communications Officer (Connor Logan) began making the international notifications.

Within four minutes, he established contact with the several agencies who could help, including: the United States Coast Guard, the French Coast Guard, His Majesty's Coast Guard in England, the United Kingdom's Maritime and Coastguard Agency's Coordination Center, and police stations in Dover, England. This guy was good."

"I'd say that both those guys were great," offered Alice.

"Dover Police, the ones in England that is, said that only 15 minutes and 48 seconds after the initial call, the maritime and coastguard agency confirmed that rescuers were underway and soon thereafter the man's brother and others had been rescued."

"Wow, so much for using search engines on the internet to get your phone numbers," said Alice.

The antenna was wired up but before they left the roof they had one more mission.

"Speaking of emergency rescues at sea."

"Multi-tasking," the folks who study the human brain are telling us, "is a myth," Liza said authoritatively. "But sequential-tasking is for real and the only way we can get all our work done around here. So please hand me that new toy I brought up in the electronics bag."

Alice handed Liza what looked like a bat bag the baseball players always seemed to be dragging on and off a baseball field. It was not unlike every sailor's sea bag.

Liza reached in and pulled out a new product that needed testing, a pneumatic line thrower using compressed gas instead of explosives (a safer and more cost effective propellant than rockets).

"This contraption is reportedly the modern answer to a monkey fists[45] and feeder lines," said Liza.

Liza had seen rocket propelled line throwers (LTA's) in her past, necessary when a ship couldn't get close enough for a manual toss of a monkey fist with attached feeder line to reach its target. But the concern with lighting a rocket from the deck of a tanker with myriad chemical fumes in the vicinity was obvious. Saving a life but setting your ship on fire in the process was a poor trade-off.

But this device utilized a compressed air capsule similar to what activates a life-saving vest to supply the thrust. It could be connected to one of nine separate specialty heads depending upon the application, unlike the weighted rope knot that head mariners have had to depend on for centuries.

The monkey fists had caught many a longshoreman unawares over the years occasionally causing head injuries and the LTA's had only a three-year life and required routine crew training to operate.

The pneumatic line throwing (PLT) device[46] is far more accurate than a sailor's heave, can be thrown (shot) a lot further, and has proven to be far more accurate. Unlike LTA's it had no OSHA or Coast Guard crew training requirements and no life limits.

Manufacturers were claiming the device, properly cared for, could be used for routine dockage as well as emergencies for decades.

Liza lined up an empty parking lot area from her rooftop perch and fired. The attachment with its connected messenger line flew much further than she could have ever heaved it, and landed cleanly where it was aimed.

They both smiled and concurred that the product "was worthy."

Sandra was pleased with herself that she had not prematurely deployed all her consultants, as Mike was needed now to fly offshore to a just occurring crisis.

A ferry dock had just collapsed on Sapelo Island, Georgia, killing at least seven people and injuring several others.

The collapse happened during Cultural Day, an annual festival celebrating the island's Gullah-Geechee community, descendants of enslaved Africans. At least 20 people fell into the Atlantic Ocean during the accident.

The Georgia Department of Natural Resources (DNR) confirmed the gangway collapse around 4 p.m., with officials first looking into whether a boat had collided with the dock.

However, authorities later confirmed that there was no collision, and the cause of the collapse remained unknown. Emergency agencies, including the U.S. Coast Guard, arrived immediately with helicopters and sonar-equipped boats to search for survivors.

Per the department sources, one of the victims was a Georgia chaplain. Six others were seriously injured, with two being evacuated to nearby hospitals for treatment. Rescue efforts continued. Sapelo Island, located about 60 miles south of Savannah, is only accessible by boat.

One of the planes Mike kept in his turntable hanger at the Falmouth Airpark was a seaplane that he could land in an island anchorage. Sandra would make arrangements to have him picked up upon arrival.

The ferry dock collapsed at the state-run ferry port, where guests were preparing to board after the festival. The ferry operates several times daily, transporting residents and visitors between the island and the mainland.

In response to the collapse, Vice President Kamala Harris, who was in Georgia for her presidential campaign, expressed her condolences, saying that she and her husband were "praying for all those who were killed or injured" and that federal support would be available if needed.

President Joe Biden and Georgia Governor Brian Kemp both expressed sympathies, with Biden stating that he and First Lady Jill Biden were "mourning the lives lost" while assisting local authorities.

The festival's organizers, the Sapelo Island Cultural and Revitalization Society, described the event's unfortunate turn as "heartbreaking." They asked the public to pray for the victims' families and expressed gratitude for their show of support.

The Georgia DNR confirmed that the dock has since been secured and that investigations into the cause of the collapse are still underway.

With all due respect to the President, Vice President, and other politicians, now offering their thoughts, prayers, and claims of support, what was needed far more was a set of unbiased eyes on how this happened. Law enforcement boats equipped with side-scan sonar and helicopter, Mike understood, were already on scene looking for missing individuals.

Sandra and Mike had, at best, marginal confidence that whatever the State of Georgia would consider being an open and nonpolitical "accident investigation" would never be that.

If Georgia knew how to keep their dirty politics out of processes like investigations it would be news to Attorney General Fani Willis and everybody else who followed recent Georgia politics.

This was a state that not only put a thumb on the scales of justice, they set up a cot for an 800 pound gorilla to sleep on a corner of that same scale.

So Mike had every reason to, and would, cooperate with local authorities of course, but his mission was to independently prepare a CSI assessment and make plans to communicate these findings to those important contacts and clients in CSI's bridge building, construction, and architectural communities.

Mike was sure that his results would be conflicting with whatever was destined to emerge a year or three from now in an "**OFFICIAL**," slick, three-ring heavily indexed, leather bound, report, that will inevitably blame the weather, un-sue able wild animals, an act-of-God, old age of the structure or a political opponent, for the entire bridge collapse.

As Alice and Liza were finishing up their rooftop satellite wiring and modern monkey fist line throwing at Cliff Safety, Inc. in San

Francisco they both spotted something rather unusual on the local shoreline. They vowed to check it out.

To their surprise, and to the surprise of many California beachgoers, millions of tiny, blue creatures known as "by-the-wind sailors," or Velella velella[47], were washing up. They found later that these sightings had been replicated on beaches from Oregon to California.

The flood of Velella colonies, which are hydrozoans, shocked and thrilled beachgoers, who started capturing and sharing the creatures on social media.

Despite their tiny size, these naturally occurring sailors traveled in colonies with a sail-like fin that caught the wind, allowing them to travel the vast expanses of the Pacific Ocean. While their emergence is a regular occurrence, the large number being seen this spring is getting them new attention.

Velella spend most of their lives wandering in the ocean currents, using their tentacles to gather food. They are not harmful to humans, but their sting can cause discomfort for zooplankton and fish larvae.

Their bright blue color serves several functions, including possibly helping them disguise themselves from predatory organisms such as ocean sunfish and providing UV protection. Researchers were constantly discovering the mysteries of these organisms, such as their life cycles and ecological impact. They travel extensively over the Pacific gyre, with their numbers undergoing fluctuations determined by food availability.

These cycles have resulted in large-scale beaching, such as the current one.

Climate change will likely bring more Velella colonies ashore, which could impact fish populations and other marine creatures.

The world's waters are getting warmer, which means these sea creatures may continue to enthrall beachgoers, but their existence also reminds us of the complicated ecosystems in our seas.

Alice took a couple of the washed ashore blue Velella for the Cliff laboratory that William was considering taking responsibility for developing out. No word on that one yet. She had heard an office rumor that his love life was a factor.

Time would tell, she guessed.

Chapter 22

Claus was working out an algorithm that he could maintain in an ongoing spreadsheet with a USA town map that would compare new arrivals of workers into each small town, midsized city, and metropolis; as a percent of existing populations. Once completed, maybe that could stem some false information being disseminated by those with less than honorable intentions.

Claus, not a native American himself but a European *washashore*, had studied 2024 America more than even committed urban planners had and knew the country well. He had personally travelled to and through all the states and had evidence of how sparsely populated much of the country now was. With abandoned buildings and storefronts being the norm in most places rather than the exception, it was clear that, population wise, America's heyday was in the past and that all of these towns of every size needed a rush of new rebuilding energy from the backbones of people who were willing to put in that effort.

Those backbones didn't seem to be the ones of a lot of the offspring of today's average Americans, too many of whom were satisfied to live in mom's basement, playing video games, and complaining that the $100,000 job offer they were entitled to hadn't come in that day's mail. Entrepreneurship wasn't even in the vocabulary of most of today's American youth.

So when Claus heard on the conservative (was there any other kind?) radio channel the statement that about 12 million people had come across the southern border under President Biden's Administration, 4% of the population, too many and too fast, he got to thinking.

As of February 22, 2024, according to the House GOP, so the Republican Party's figures, since Joe Biden took office and enacted his **"failed far left open borders agenda,"** there had been over **"7.2 million** illegal immigrants" who have entered the United States through our Southern Border.

So 12 million is probably not accurate, but whatever. That's but 3.6% by their actual number, or 2% if the GOP's alternative numbers are correct.

The United States is under-populated and losing working age population, so increasing our population by 2 to 4% with people who are mostly of working age is a big gift to our economy.

The only way to keep our economy growing is to have more people in the labor force, and with Baby Boomers aging out, and fewer young people coming along, we would be much worse off without more immigration.

The problem is that we define these willing workers as "illegals." If we made their presence in our country legal, it would be a huge win-win for us and for them (though a loss for their own countries, who would be losing the most ambitious and optimistic people).

Compare our population density to the UK for example, if "under-populated" seems wrong:

US: 94 people per square mile (If you take out Alaska and Hawaii, it's 111 people/sq mi.)

UK: 720 people/sq mi

The UK is not an over-populated hell-hole! It also has lots of agriculture and open space.

So the US certainly has room for 7 or 12 million more people.

We do need a lot more housing—and that's a job that many immigrants are eager to do. So, Claus, frankly, did not think that America was in an immigration crisis at all.

And if the country's dark force was taken off stage (and rightly imprisoned) the country had already approved a bi-partisan bill that would have solved the name calling crisis of "illegals" versus "documented."

CAPE SAFETY, INC. - EVENTS WON'T STOP

Claus still found it amazing that the Americans yelling "illegal" at poor folks from Central America, DACA[48] kids, and mother's whose kids had been kidnapped by ICE and Homeland customs authorities, wouldn't dare to yell "illegal" at Melania Trump or her "anchor baby" Barron Trump.

Or for that matter, celebrities and sports heroes they enjoyed watching like Adele, Sting, Andrea Bocelli, Paul McCartney, the Milwaukee Bucks star Giannis Sina Ugo Antetokounmpo, the Los Angeles Dodgers star Shohei Ohtani, and most professional NHL hockey (42% Canadian) and pro circuit tennis players.

Claus couldn't remember a single incident where these celebrities faced some American redneck calling them "illegal."

Why, because it had never happened.

Punching down was far easier and apparently carried much less chance of repercussions.

Normally Claus would be engaged in macro rather than micro projects. Convincing banks and large businesses to do the right things when it came to supporting ventures that would have a positive rather than a negative effect on world populations, world employment, climate alteration, resource devastation, and if two words were needed, *end exploitation*.

If he scored himself, he'd be hard pressed to grade his results higher than a C.

But he knew without his attempts, at least, of being an advocate for the planet's conscience, these banks and conglomerates would continue to wreak havoc all in the economic interest of profitability.

One example Claus was thinking of was a recent project, the small Indonesian village of Wonorejo.

Wonorejo was once a thriving community. But when energy giant Adaro bought up land surrounding it to build coal settling ponds, families fled.

Now, Wonorejo was a ghost town where coal ash has blanketed a dilapidated school and an abandoned health post.

This form of reckless destruction by Adaro would continue if banks like JPMorgan, Citi, and Deutsche agreed to back its upcoming $750 million bond.

Claus would be one to try to talk them out of backing that bond initiative.

Adaro was single-minded in its pursuit of coal.

But maybe like the 1889 Jamestown Flood, maybe 2,000 lives could have been saved if a Claus, in that time, had convinced the magnates of the South Fork Fishing and Hunting club to trade in a bit of their leisure for the safety of the town below.

North Kalimantan rainforests, migration routes of critically-endangered Hawksbill sea turtles, and livelihoods plus the incomes of people employed in traditional agriculture, livestock, and fisheries in Indonesia were depending on it.

The growing public pressure had already compelled banks like BNP Paribas and DBS to rule out any financing or underwriting

CAPE SAFETY, INC. - EVENTS WON'T STOP

services to Adaro. So if Claus could make a successful pitch maybe he could make these banks drop Adaro as a client for good.

But if banks went ahead, Adaro would continue to flout Indonesia's commitment to fossil fuel phase-out and exacerbate environmental degradation and human rights violations.

Claus knew it could be done because he had done it before. Like when Claus had teamed with fellow Ekō[49] members to pile pressure on Deutsche Bank to end its involvement in Whitehaven Coal's bond issue. **Another day, another fight.**

Chapter 23

As much as Sandra would have liked to steer clear of the entire marine entertainment park workplace scene as a place to take a controversial position; as the lead scientist and CEO both, the responsibility was best placed on her to discuss the firm's opinion of this popular work space.

Sandra had watched the documentary movie **Blackfish**, and had just completed the David Kirby book titled, **Death at SeaWorld**, plus talked to many associates about the matter.

Distressing was the summary word that came to mind.

Videos on Youtube.com that were still accessible showed trainers being attacked and pulled to the tank bottom in more than one instance. And a couple of videos bore witness to these events turning to fatal attacks by these giant mammals who carried the reputation as *killer whales.*

Orcas weren't whales but dolphins to start with and they had no history of attacking man in the wild.

But what happened in these cases was uncontestable.

Orca captivity, shows, and displays were a giant and worldwide business that employed hundreds, maybe even thousands of people. True it was that people have long enjoyed watching the exciting interactions between trainers and these wonderful creatures performing tricks and seemingly swimming in great harmony.

But the reality didn't match the show image and these powerful beasts had good and bad moods like every other animal, seemingly exacerbated by lives in too small a space, food of various qualities depending on performance, too much inattention and boredom, and an unpredictable nature in the presence of trainers—even trainers they had worked with for years.

So the practice of capturing and displaying orcas in public aquariums and aquatic theme parks was gaining recognition for its cruelty with renewed scorn as a blatantly commercial and failed experiment, going on since 1961, that needed to be brought to conclusion.

The ends of public entertainment and "education" of the ways of these mammals was not exceeding the means of creating miserable whales and frightened trainer employees, it appeared to many observers.

Sandra's views wouldn't alter much in the business environment but her approval or disapproval of practices might carry some weight as the whale captivity controversy swirled.

OSHA over many years had tried and effectively failed to convince these oceanic theme parks to become safer places to work.

But in 2014, after a long drawn out battle with SeaWorld ownership and management, one that ended in the United States Appeals Court, the court ruled that SeaWorld had violated its employer responsibilities by exposing trainers to "recognized hazards" when working with "killer whales" and must now limit whale-human contact during its shows.

SeaWorld. the marine entertainment titan, had hoped to overturn OSHA's ruling[50] and continue allowing trainers to enter the water with the Orcas and perform dives, jumps and many other tricks.

But the death to trainer Dawn Brancheau who was pulled underwater and drowned by a 12,000 lb. orca named Tilikum in the Orlando theme park provided clear evidence to OSHA of the inherent dangers of this work. Dawn's fatality from an orca encounter wasn't the only fatality either.

Chronicled in **Death at SeaWorld** was the tremendous boredom this animal faced in captivity and the deprivations he faced including a night tank he could barely move in, and social separation from other whales for reasons disassociated with the animal's well being.

Or so Sandra had been asked to pontificate on by friends at WDC[51].

The concept of capturing animals for public display went back to ancient times when even the ancient Coliseum in Rome was built with a raised subfloor, beneath which wild animals were kept.

Maybe animal captivity had never been the best of ideas.

But certainly no one was going to get a time machine to change what had been. The only question now was what would be.

Although the highly intelligent octopuses at the New England Aquarium and elsewhere interact with visitors everyday and seem to enjoy their human friendships, was it ethically proper to keep intelligent species under human slavery, to put in tersely?

The same ethical dilemma was present with zoo and circus elephants, and certainly the full expanse of primates.

Should species intelligence be considered the difference between *guppies & goldfish* in tanks and *dolphins & octopus* in tanks?

Could the horrific cornering, harvesting, and capturing of these free ranging orcas, the slaughtering of many of them in the process, and the forever separation of them from family members and groups, ever be justified to force them into a life as human entertainers, two or three shows daily, in a SeaWorld or like exhibition park?

It would be hard for Sandra to say yes to that.

And although many visitors enjoyed touching and being touched by the aquarium octopuses, was that reason enough to take them from their natural habitats? And yes, on occasion they too had inexplicably bitten visitors with their sharp beak-like mouths. Were they also having a, *I've had enough,* moment?

Swimming alongside sharks, killer whales, and octopus may never be the natural thing to do. That is *their* home, uninvited guests, not ours.

Cutting a trapped orca free of a fish net entanglement as he beseeches you for help, sure, but paddling around him/her during a moody moment or a mating could have a far different outcome.

Such treatment of an intelligent mammal, it seemed obvious, could result in an erratic outburst from the animal with dangerous consequences. There had been evidence of same including pool tank damage and damage to other pool objects.

So the issue seemed to be focused now on whether captivity of these ocean behemoths should be continued. Experts had doubts that the orcas born in captivity without the experience of an ocean existence actually possessed the skills to fend for themselves if released back to the ocean. For their own protection, they might need to live out their lives in man-made tanks.

But the captured-then-contained orcas didn't fit that history, and a "Free Willy" future for them seemed possible.

Could that not be an equitable resolution in the interests of all?

A continuation of the practices of the past ten years with trainers and others separated at all times from the whales by physical barriers and a commitment to raise no more whales in captivity plus _catch no more orcas_ for exhibition purposes.

Granted it will put an eventual end to the last live whale at these theme parks, but to replicate that experience, daily whale watch excursions in the open oceans were still readily available from many coastal cities.

Theme parks had planning time now to adjust for that eventuality by investing instead in virtual technologies for customer experiences that could also do far more to incorporate oceanographic educational elements that the "killer whale shows" honestly had very little of.

Throughout America, CSI had spent close to half a century making jobs safer for the people who did them. Workers at marine theme parks deserved nothing less than that.

What was once an acceptable work practice like reaching hands into printing presses, walking skyscraper beams with no tie-offs, using explosives inside underground mines, riding high speed fire engines while only grasping a hand strap, entering ship bilges without testing the air for available oxygen, or leaping off the noses of 12,000 pound Orcas to entertain others was now "old school."

No longer did we have horses leaping off high diving boards in Coney Island and soon we would no longer have massive orcas in small man-made tanks performing tricks for their dinners either.

Changes.

Chapter 24

Mike had flown back from his bridge investigation in Mendenhall, Mississippi, had parked the plane in his turntable then took his Boomerbuggy to the headquarters from the Airpark. It was the latest toy he was trying out and so far he was pleased with it. The mobility scooter, as it was called, was climate controlled, both heating and air conditioning. The enclosed cabin shielded him from rain, wind, and anything else that might try to dampen his spirits.

It could reach speeds of up to 12 mph and the long-lasting battery gave him a range of 37.2 miles, far less than his trip to headquarters, where he could recharge it for his trip back home. Power windows, power sun roof, with a full-color LED display with a rear backup camera.

Mike loved transportation toys.

Mike's preliminary investigation into the cause of the Georgia collapse he had yet to reveal. The gangway had been secured and transported to a specialized facility where the Georgia Bureau of Investigation (GBI) and the Critical Incident Reconstruction (CIR) team of the Georgia DNR (Department of Natural Resources) would reportedly be doing their own detailed analysis.

People in the know had far more confidence in what Mike would put into his report than what all these folks working with the various acronym departments would come out with.

Snake, Lars, and Claus all caught him as he walked in the door and even before robot East Sweepster could grab his coat and hand him a coffee, each consultant was peppering Mike with questions, and telling him about their own recent projects.

Naturally, Tickets the Cape dog met Mike, too, expecting his treats. He got some.

Lars' news story about a recent discovery of *how life on Earth actually began* looked to be the story that trumped the rest. Scientific findings of life's origins tended to get one's immediate attention.

Dark oxygen, a newly discovered form of oxygen deep within the Pacific Ocean was rewriting our scientific understanding of how oxygen is produced.

Photosynthetic organisms like plants and algae use energy from sunlight to create the planet's oxygen, but new evidence, published by Nature Geoscience, had just shown how oxygen is also produced in complete darkness at the seafloor 4,000 meters below the ocean surface, where no light can penetrate.

The Scottish Association for Marine Science (SAMS) had been the team making the discovery studying metal nodules that contained metals such as manganese, nickel and cobalt, which are required to produce lithium-ion batteries for electric vehicles and mobile phones.

In the exploration it was found that nodules carrying a very high electrical charge can lead to the splitting of seawater into hydrogen and oxygen in a process called seawater electrolysis. It was about the voltage of a simple AA battery. So when nodules are clustered together significant voltages could result.

The discovery proved that the long understood theory that oxygen could only be generated through photosynthesis wasn't true.

But around half of the Earth's oxygen comes from the ocean[1], states the National Oceanic and Atmospheric Administration, NOAA.

Scientists formerly attributed the production to the following:

- ◈ Oceanic plankton[2]
- ◈ Drifting plants
- ◈ Algae
- ◈ Some bacteria

But all of these organisms listed are capable of photosynthesis, thus creating oxygen. But since they wouldn't be able to do that so deep underwater life there must be supported, at least augmented by nodule generated oxygen.

How that presently affects deepwater sea life has yet to be studied.

And mining these modules would surely remove them from what might be life support for such marine life that lives its full life in these great depths.

1. https://oceanservice.noaa.gov/facts/ocean-oxygen.html#_853ae90f0351324bd73ea615e6487517__4c761f170e016836ff84498202b99827__853ae90f0351324bd73ea615e6487517_text_43ec3e5dee6e706af7766fffea512721_Scientists_0bcef9c45bd8a48eda1b26eb0c61c869_20estimate_0bcef9c45bd8a48eda1b26eb0c61c869_20that_0bcef9c45bd8a48eda1b26eb0c61c869_20roughly_0bcef9c45bd8a48eda1b26eb0c61c869_20half_c0cb5f0fcf239ab3d9c1fcd31fff1efc_smallest_0bcef9c45bd8a48eda1b26eb0c61c869_20photosynthetic_0bcef9c45bd8a48eda1b26eb0c61c869_20organism_0bcef9c45bd8a48eda1b26eb0c61c869_20on_0bcef9c45bd8a48eda1b26eb0c61c869_20Earth.

2. https://oceanservice.noaa.gov/facts/plankton.html

Just the activity of mining these nodules can create toxic sediment plumes unique to ocean mining that have been shown to suffocate, starve and poison marine life, also.

A small scale 2-hour mining experiment on the Takuyo-Daiichi off the eastern coast of Japan caused fish and shrimp populations to drop by 43% in the immediate mining area and 56% in surrounding areas.

In the case of these polymetallic nodules—the primary extraction of modern deep sea mining—mining vehicles not unlike tractors plowing a field, would collect these nodules along with disrupting the surface of these sea beds. The nodules would then be piped up to the surface vessel for processing and any waste such as sediments and other organic materials would be pumped back into the water.

While the deep sea was once thought to be devoid of life—too dark, cold, and starved of food for anything to survive—we now knew that it was the largest habitable space on the planet and home to a dazzling array of life, most still unknown to mankind. To date, tens of thousands of species have been found there with estimates that there may be a million more. In the Clarion-Clipperton Zone alone, where 17 mining companies have already divided their spoils on paper, researchers have recently discovered over 5,000 species that were previously unknown to science.

The Pacific Island nation of Nauru wants to begin mining in international waters now.

The 168 member nations that comprise the UN International Seabed Authority (ISA), has not yet authorized this request and is still developing deep-sea mining regulations.

Norway has already initiated a process to open its own waters for the exploration of deep sea mineral resources.

Some nations, such as Norway and Nauru, are leading the charge for exploration and extraction; other countries such as Germany and Canada as well as the European Parliament have called for national and regional moratoria.

CAPE SAFETY, INC. - EVENTS WON'T STOP

Seventeen deep mining contractors were awaiting the go ahead in the Clarion-Clipperton Zone in the Pacific Ocean, an area rich in deposits.

Mike was aware that several studies had concluded that there was no shortage of high tech needed mineral resources on land, but those too, like the human exploitation happening in the Congo, presented ongoing S, H, and E concerns.

So Lars' news was scientifically significant but not course changing for Cape Safety, Inc.

More deaths of desperately poor African children, women, and men while mining in deep underground tunnels for Belgian billionaires in inhuman conditions[52]; or more sea life destruction?

Unacceptable choices the UN needed to address and improve before either choice was made, thought Mike.

African cobalt and minerals mining could be done far more safely but the high technology exploiters like Cisco, Apple, and Google needed to stop taking advantage of these economically distressed societies.

And what difference the new energy and oxygen discovery could make to the world?

No one knew yet.

So certainly racing to extract what, maybe, should be left in place seemed strategically dicey to Mike as well.

Let the 17 big ocean mining firms better justify their takings before granting any permissions. What about the silting? We had mining industry assurances that there would be no damage with strip mining. What a disaster that had been ecologically.

Mining firms throughout history hadn't shown much ecological responsibility and it was pretty doubtful that they were now suddenly serious about becoming environmentally responsible.

Maggie had another year or two before retirement and had spent it all "homeported" in Woods Hole. Sandra would love it if she spent the rest of her term helping out Sue, Alice, Liza, and maybe William too, staff out the Cliff Safety Inc. operation in San Francisco.

As another winter season approached and she once again dragged out the L.L. Bean flannel shirts, fleece vests, and Bean boots, Maggie was *warming* to the idea of a warm California winter instead of the usual.

She watched as two seagulls flew past on a guano diving run that missed her by not that much. Woods Hole for years back in time was a guano sanctuary. So much so the biggest enterprise on the Cape for a while was the Woods Hole Guano Factory providing fertilizer to southeastern Massachusetts farmers. Eventually the entrepreneur owner decided to invest big in the Cape Cod Railroad, primarily as a way to get his product off the Cape and into the hands of even distant farmers.

In the 1850's guano was a far bigger American business and was gathered from as far as the islands of the Gulf of California, and shipped to, among other places, England and Germany.

Guano, bird and bat droppings are full of nitrogen. It smells bad as one would imagine, but it helps a lot of stuff grow big and tall. Sellers long claimed that the cost of their product would be far less than the additional yields they would receive and there was little blowback on that claim.

Many nations like the United States and Great Britain annexed small islands simply for the access to the island's guano. Where they couldn't buy the island outright, negotiations gave these nations the access they wanted. In dry regions like the Gulf of California, bird droppings accumulate over time to several feet thick, or more. Some "rock islands" were more guano than rock.

Mining was far more than a couple of guys with poor olfactory responses with a couple of shovels. Some contracts called for five thousand tons of guano a year and operations fully capable of removing 10,000 tons of guano from a single location.

But then the bottom fell out of the guano market. First potassium nitrate, or salt peter, found its way into the world's fertilizer market. Not all that much later in 1913 the invention of what became known as the Haber-Bosch process allowed large scale relatively inexpensive synthesis of nitrogen fertilizers[53]. With less need for the back breaking guano mining in terrible working conditions with low wages the "trade" quickly morphed into a job from history. Not many looked back on it nostalgically. And the peninsula that contained the smelly guano factory was now home to mansions worth millions of dollars to one worth $25 million.

Yes, it was a far bigger business at one time than Maggie's guano operation of collecting a cup full to help out her window boxes.

As she pulled her collar tight, tied the drawstrings, then pulled up her hood, she said to nobody but herself, "Yeah, no guano", maybe it was time for this empty nester to fly west herself.

Chapter 25

Emergency Services had always been an area of concern to Cape Safety, Inc.

Work*man*'s Compensation started in 1911 and was the term used for that type of workplace medical and lost wages insurance when CSI came onto the scene to help.

But since then the "new" (25 years old now) term was Work*ers* Compensation coverage. Every American company was required by law to provide that coverage for its workforce.

But prompt medical response to every injury was still the best way to mitigate the damage and get the worker healthy once again. The faster and the better the initial care the easier it was for the emergency room medics to do their trauma magic.

Most American towns still relied on EMT-trained firefighters responding with the closest available truck to provide that initial intervention. It worked, but using the town ladder truck or pumper truck to respond to an old timer who "fell and couldn't get up" was, in no one's view, the perfect approach to providing emergency medical assistance.

Now a program credited with reducing trips to emergency rooms and saving patients and emergency services more than $700,000 over the past 20 months was just significantly expanding in East County, down San Diego way.

El Cajon became the first city in the state to participate in the **nurse navigator program** when it was launched as El Cajon Community Care in 2023. La Mesa and Lemon Grove joined in 2024 under the name East County **EMS Nurse Navigation Program**, and Santee soon will join along with other areas within the Grossmont Healthcare District's sphere of influence, including San Diego County Fire Protection District, San Miguel Consolidated Fire Protection District, Alpine Fire Protection District, Lakeside Fire Protection

District, Bonita-Sunnyside Fire Protection and the service areas of the Viejas, Sycuan and Barona Indian reservations' fire departments.

The expansion will see the program grow from serving about 100,000 people in El Cajon to 600,000 residents in East County, making it one of the largest communities in the nation to participate in the program.

Under the program, 911 calls are answered by the Heartland Communications Facility Authority, where dispatchers ask a series of questions to determine the seriousness of the caller's situation.

Most calls result in a medical crew dispatched to assist the person, who then may require a trip to an emergency room. *Others' calls are forwarded to Texas, where they will talk with a California-licensed nurse trained to manage 911 medical calls.*

Hearing a "y'all" response in a California crisis probably won't be too jarring over time as we all needed to get comfortable with an India dialect when calling what we thought was our downtown cable service.

The new approach can reduce the number of patients in emergency rooms, free up crews to respond to more calls, save wear and tear on fire department resources and save patients thousands of dollars in medical bills.

"It helps the transport agencies, but really the biggest help is to the caller, because they're getting the most appropriate care," Heartland Fire & Rescue Chief Bent Koch said where the expansion was announced.

The expansion comes at a time when El Cajon is considering charging licensed care facilities in the city for what officials consider an excessive number of 911 calls for non-medical emergencies, despite having the nurse navigator program in place.

The program could have a bigger impact in El Cajon next year, as more calls are expected to be diverted to nurse navigators.

Paul Forney, regional director of the ambulance service American Medical Response, said just 7% of calls were diverted to nurses since the program's launch in El Cajon, but that is expected to increase to 10% or 15% as the program reaches maturity in another year.

Paul Larimore, director of Emergency Services and Critical Care at Sharp Grossmont Hospital, said the program could provide some much-needed relief at emergency rooms. At Sharp, the number of ER patients increased by 5,000 over the past year to reach about 180,000, he said.

According to data from American Medical Response, the program generated savings of about $735,000 in El Cajon over the past 20 months by avoiding emergency care cost, including for patients, the city and responders.

Of 776 callers who were connected to a nurse navigator, 38% did not require an emergency response or visit to an ER, 31% were treated in their own home, 21% were treated with nurse advice only, 5% were treated with virtual telehealth care, 5% were treated with a visit from a mobile urgent care unit, 5% were directed to an alternative destination such as an urgent care, 43% required a not-time-sensitive response from AMR and 15% required basic life support, a response without lights and sirens from emergency medical technicians rather than paramedics.

Just 30 of the 776 calls required a traditional 911 advanced life support response after the nurses determined their condition was more serious than originally appeared.

The Nurse Navigator program was launched in Washington, D.C. in 2018 by Global Medical Response, owner of American Medical Response. The program is in nine states, with new California participants planned for Contra Costa, Santa Clara, Stanislaus and Riverside counties.

As technology and AI grow it will be incumbent on Americans to put it to the best uses possible. Uses like this are an example.

Our technologies need worthier uses than better POKEMON "gaming" experiences, superimposing faces on suggestive photos,[54] and other crap.

People intelligent enough to program with such technology are our high technology gatekeepers.

Gatekeepers who need to be spending their time and energy helping this artificial knowledge make the world a better place not just a richer place, a more fascist place, or a cruder and ruder place[55].

Chapter 26

GCaptain.com, a great source of timely nautical information to Cape and Cliff, had just published what could best be described as maybe "a cautionary Tale" about the cruise industry and life aboard for both crew and passengers.

As the article's author, Captain John Konrad, saw it, the open sea calls, exotic ports tempt, and buffets overflow—perhaps cultivating a microbial zoo in your gut. As you step aboard, a question lingers like a questionable odor: How clean is this ship? Are those gleaming handrails just polished metal, or a slick of sunscreen and sneezes? Is that sea mist or someone's ill-timed cough spraying your face? The allure of cruising is undeniable, but so is the microscopic army plotting a mutiny against your immune system before you even set sail.

Not all cruise lines are equal when it comes to battling the microscopic stowaways that can turn a dream vacation into a gastrointestinal nightmare.

The Centers for Disease Control and Prevention (CDC) know this all too well.

While they officially ended their COVID-19 precautions in July 2022[1], their inspectors have still been making unannounced visits to these floating resorts, clipboard in hand, eyes peeled for any breach in the bulwark against bacteria and viruses.

So far, said Konrad, 19 ships have risen to the occasion, earning perfect scores in the CDC's rigorous Vessel Sanitation Program[2].

These vessels are the shining beacons of cleanliness in an industry often shadowed by tales of norovirus[56] outbreaks and less-than-sterile conditions.

First, Konrad offered, the Cleanest Cruise Ships in 2024.

---

1. https://gcaptain.com/cdc-ends-cruise-ship-covid-19-program/
2. https://www.cdc.gov/vessel-sanitation/about/index.html

Here's the roster[3]:

◈ *Carnival Spirit*—Carnival Cruise Line (inspected September 3)
◈ *Viking Orion*—Viking Ocean Cruises (inspected August 18)
◈ *Seabourn Odyssey*—Seabourn Cruise Line (inspected August 16)
◈ *Norwegian Jewel*—Norwegian Cruise Line (inspected July 24)
◈ *Oceania Regatta*—Oceania Cruises (inspected July 24)
◈ *Radiance of the Seas*—Royal Caribbean International (inspected July 21)
◈ *MSC Meraviglia*—MSC Cruises (inspected July 9)
◈ *Norwegian Bliss*—Norwegian Cruise Line (inspected June 22)
◈ *MSC Seashore*—MSC Cruises (inspected May 26)
◈ *Norwegian Sky*—Norwegian Cruise Line (inspected May 23)
◈ *Brilliance of the Seas*—Royal Caribbean International (inspected May 16)
◈ *Viking Polaris*—Viking Cruises (inspected April 2)
◈ *Celebrity Equinox*—Celebrity Cruises (inspected February 25)
◈ *Norwegian Breakaway*—Norwegian Cruise Line (inspected February 25)
◈ *Norwegian Escape*—Norwegian Cruise Line (inspected January 27)
◈ *Explora I*—MSC Cruises (inspected January 25)
◈ *Disney Fantasy*—Disney Cruise Line (inspected January 24)

---

3. https://wwwn.cdc.gov/inspectionquerytool/inspectionwith100score.aspx

◇ *Celebrity Ascent*—Celebrity Cruises (inspected January 7)

◇ *Norwegian Gem*—Norwegian Cruise Line (inspected January 2)

But while these ships fly the flag of sanitation excellence, the sea isn't entirely calm.

The CDC has reported 10 bacterial and viral outbreaks on cruise ships this year, most of them courtesy of the notorious Norwalk Virus. That's fewer than the 14 outbreaks logged in 2023, but numbers can be cold comfort if you're the one confined to your cabin, acquainting yourself with the nearest restroom.

Half of these outbreaks have occurred on ships from Royal Caribbean Group's main line and its Celebrity Cruises subsidiary.

The *Radiance of the Seas* had the misfortune of hosting not one but two outbreaks this year—first norovirus, then a bout of salmonella. It's a stark reminder that even with stringent measures; the microscopic world doesn't easily yield.

Norovirus is the uninvited guest that just won't leave. Highly contagious, it thrives in the close quarters of cruise ships, spreading through contaminated food, water, surfaces, and person-to-person contact. Symptoms like vomiting, diarrhea, nausea, and stomach pain can sideline even the most enthusiastic traveler.

The CDC's Vessel Sanitation Program is the industry's sentinel against such adversities. Inspectors arrive unannounced, scrutinizing every nook and cranny. Kitchens, pools, children's play areas—all are under the microscope. They're not just looking for the obvious culprits like vermin or improperly stored food. They delve into the minutiae: Is the hair and lint strainer in the pool being disinfected often enough? Is the dishwasher reaching the necessary temperatures to obliterate germs?

Out of 119 ships inspected this year, the majority scored above 95. That's encouraging, but perfection is a high bar. Last year by this time, 29 ships had achieved a perfect score; by year's end, 34 had. The drop to 19 this year might raise an eyebrow, but perhaps it's a testament to more rigorous inspections rather than declining standards.

Despite the cruise industry's strides toward higher sanitation standards, several ships have fallen short in the CDC's Vessel Sanitation Program inspections for 2024.

According to the CDC's Green Sheet[4] the most glaring case is the *Hanseatic Inspiration*, which received a score of **62**—the lowest among the inspected vessels.

Other ships like the *Kydon, Evrima, Caribbean Princess,* and *Carnival Breeze* each scored **86**, which is below the industry average but not terrible scores and could indicate notable deficiencies in the health plan, crew training or other factors besides germs and dirt.

Conversely they could be inconsistent sanitation practices, lapses in cleaning procedures, or failures in adhering to proper hygiene standards among the crew.

Konrad encourages all to *"check the CDC website for reports for individual ships before you make judgments."*

So what ships are the "Nastiest" ships of 2024?

He also listed the lowest-rated cruise ships based on the provided CDC inspection scores:

1. *Hanseatic Inspiration—Inspected on 09/29/2024*—**Score: 62**
Received the lowest score in the provided list.
2. *Kydon—Inspected on 09/04/2023*—**Score: 86**
Ro-Ro Ferry Class *cruise*.
3. *Evrima—Inspected on 02/09/2024*—**Score: 86**
Ritz-Carlton Yacht[5] Collection

---

4. https://wwwn.cdc.gov/inspectionquerytool/InspectionGreenSheetRpt.aspx

4. *Caribbean Princess*—Inspected on 03/20/2024—**Score: 86**
Below Princess fleet average.
5. *Carnival Breeze*—Inspected on 03/21/2024—**Score: 86**
Below Carnival fleet average.
6. *MSC Magnifica*—Inspected on 05/17/2024—**Score: 86**
Below MSC Fleet Average

7. *Carnival Miracle*—Inspected on 04/21/2024—**Score: 88**
8. *National Geographic Sea Bird*—Inspected on 07/25/2024—**Score: 88**
9. *Adventure of the Seas*—Inspected on 01/23/2024—**Score: 89**
10. *Aurora* -—Inspected on 9/18/2023 -—**Score: 89**
11. *Crystal Serenity*—Inspected on 02/03/2024—**Score: 89**
12. *Carnival Elation*—Inspected on 03/14/2024—**Score: 89**

The cruise industry is navigating tricky waters. Balancing the luxury and freedom that passengers expect with the invisible battle against pathogens is no small feat.

But the decrease in outbreaks suggests progress. Enhanced sanitation protocols, staff training, and perhaps a heightened awareness among passengers about hand hygiene are all playing a part, but these measures cost money . . . money some lines seem more willing to invest than others.

Konrad ends his article by suggesting, "So next time you consider setting sail, perhaps give a nod to those ships that have made the CDC's honor roll."

CSI consultants had few illusions that people would be picking their next cruises following this advice, no matter how the Communications Center managed to amp it up.

---

5. https://gcaptain.com/ritz-carlton-launches-ilma-worlds-largest-hotel-branded-superyacht/

But we had to hope.

Cape Safety, Inc. had been working with the cruise shipping industry for years on another big problem[57] that despite their help was continuing.

Allure of the Seas, another of Royal Caribbean's super cruise ships, had just reported another passenger overboard overnight with no witnesses. Was it a passenger suicide or a tragic accident? It was the 418th person overboard from a cruise ship since 2000.

Too much free booze, too few passenger barricades, and insufficient passenger monitoring, were all found by CSI during their recent study to be contributing factors to this statistic. What factors fit here? Maybe time would tell but more likely we would never know.

Should some form of psychological evaluation need to precede cruise ship ticket buying? Should the cruise ships invest in psychologists or psychiatrists as crew members? Remember, these ships are carrying upwards of 5,000 passengers on their routine voyages now.

These were just a few of the questions OSHA and the United States Coast guard needed to be asking these billion dollar shipping companies, whether American companies or not.

It was the American taxpayer's dollars that inevitably go into extensive United States Coast Guard Search and Rescue posture with every one of these 418 incidents. Is that fair or should the cruise ship be billed for that search and have to add it to their costs of doing business?

Chapter 27

Why do so many people still follow a charlatan? thought Megan. She was the consultant with the unfortunate last name of, Abuck, a name that was so contrary to her character.

Megan-a-buck had never been one of Megan's character traits. She had the modest bank account to prove it too.

But working for improvement to the lives of others was what she had done with her career rather than accumulating wealth and she was plenty proud of that.

It was almost sad that so many people with only a riches focus can't take any of their wealth with them when they died, but alas, that was everyone's fate.

Yet a few of her friends, and not ones doing poorly, just ones that apparently thought they should have been rewarded better by whatever sell-out career they had chosen, still blamed the world for what they couldn't yet acquire, as though more "stuff" was the only goal of life.

Just that morning, Megan once again had to defend Vice President and Presidential candidate Kamala Harris's record on the economy and her border policies to these same friends who always expected more.

It was disheartening to her that these associates were even considering voting for the alternative ballot choice, a 34-count convicted felon with an additional rape conviction and a campaign of fascist pronouncements who was melting down daily as over 37 psychiatrists[58] identified a clear diagnosis of dementia and cognitive impairment.

And even her recitation of facts didn't appear to move their needles even a *scosh*.

That was discouraging.

The economy under Biden was the strongest in the world, we have had more than 16 million jobs created with record GDP and stock market growth and the border showed 5 times as many people had been refused admittance under Biden than under Trump and 3 times as many deportations. Harris had even met with Central American leaders to help thrash out a Central American economic improvement package that would encourage many of their own people to stay in their home countries and not make that dangerous trek to the Mexican border. Walking trips over hundreds of miles with small children and babies in arms was a miserable thing for these people, contrary to the words of MAGA mouthpieces who acted as though they were coming to our borders on a weekend lark.

Oh, Megan also gave them a statistic much closer to her heart that over 2,000 companies left the United States when Trump was President taking their jobs with them thanks to his inept trade wars and the "tariffs" Trump still didn't understand.

NO FOREIGNERS PAY TARIFFS. It should be written on billboards and every high school and college whiteboard, she thought.

But the press, who had been no friend to the Harris campaign in 2024, still kept the contest neck and neck to keep ratings and readers high only a couple of weeks before voting day.

If Megan hadn't been so industrial hygiene savvy, and a classy woman to boot, she might have *spit* in exasperation.

She didn't and wouldn't.

Now even the thought of that, as she glanced at the tiny covering of fall snow that had fallen the night before, got her brain fired up once again to the history of that appalling practice. Hygiene had the oddest of evolutions.

Reportedly, in "days of yore," there was prevalence on virgin snow like this, tavern floors, hotel carpets, nearly everywhere of expectorated chewing tobacco.

American men, so the history noted, seemed determined to mark every standing object with tobacco juice, despite the numerous spittoons left out for collection.

British visitors invariably found the habit appalling.

Before Charles Dickens set out on his 1842 tour of America, he'd heard stories from other travelers about the country's obsession with chewing tobacco but assumed such accounts were overblown.

But he found they were true.

"The thing itself is an exaggeration of nastiness, which cannot be outdone. In all the public places of America this filthy custom is recognized. In the courts of law the judge has his spittoon, the crier his, the witness his, and the prisoner his; while the jurymen and spectators are provided for, as so many men who in course of nature must desire to spit incessantly."[59]

Target spitting appeared to be a particular preoccupation, although one at which few men were adept, judging from the splatters of brown spit that marked the terrain in front and around spittoons, fireplace hearths, and lamp posts.

"I was surprised to observe," Dickens wrote further, "that even steady old chewers of great experience are not always good marksmen, which has rather inclined me to doubt that general proficiency with the rifle, of which we have heard so much in England."

Yup, and Americans and their guns was another matter, as Megan Abuck went through her inbox for her next real, not mental, mission.

Chapter 28

Mike had a helicopter he flew fairly regularly for enjoyment and once to help some cranberry grower friends wash the floating berries into a waiting collection boom for harvesting.

But electrical lines he purposely flew well clear of. Marker balls on those power lines even gave out proximity warnings so there was little excuse to get too near them.

Aerial utility work using helicopters was a different animal.

It seemed like the ultimate in high hazard professions.

Nobody would ever say that it wasn't up there in the top ten at least.

But the electrical utility sector had a remarkably good safety record and by no means was that by luck and good fortune.

Since 1947 when helicopter support of the industry began, safety protocols, equipment, and procedures have been the only way that work has been performed.

Combining the inherent dangers of flying any aircraft plus close proximity to highest voltages of electricity has been and continues to be the work of serious, highly trained personnel only.

The first step of such a safety system approach to mitigating the risks of this work was defining the operational environment and outlining the hazards associated with each flight profile.

The fact that you don't see this type of work being performed in high winds, thunderstorms, the dark of night, or blizzard conditions is no coincidence. Hazard mitigation is complex, but not challenging weather conditions unnecessarily is hazard control 101.

SWP's or safe work procedures are step-by-step instructions on how to perform a particular task and are used religiously, not to meet an OSHA standard but because the work is no place for improvisation.

- Minimum approach distances are followed, **always**
- Proper and properly tested personal protective equipment is used, **always**
- Helicopters are pre-tripped and well inspected by licensed aerial mechanics, **always**
- If changes to operations, procedures, or equipment are necessary they are discussed among all workers involved, SWP's are altered, and everyone is on the new page, **always**.
- This environment is not where the left hand doesn't know what the right hand is doing, **always**.

An SMS is based on leadership and accountability.

The best hazard assessment is always done pro-actively; not reactively after a glitch shows itself.

Prior to flight the pilot performs the flight risk assessment utilizing the flight risk assessment tool (FRAT) that includes the number of consecutive days the pilot has been on duty and his (her) experience.

The FRAT is scored for total risk based on the answers given by the pilot.

- If the total risk score is determined to be low, the pilot is good to go.
- If the total risk score is determined to elevated, the pilot mitigates the risk factors and is then allowed to fly.

- If the total risk score is determined to be moderate, the pilot shall contact the chief pilot or safety director to discuss the mitigation plan.
- If the total risk score is determined to be high, the pilot shall stop. The flight is not allowed to commence until the risk can be eliminated.

Each flight includes a tailboard (huddle, toolbox, lunch pail - depending on your industry term) meeting at the landing pad between all air and ground crew involved.

The FAA has established criteria for human external cargo (HEC) operations that also need to be understood and respected. No one else who isn't essential to that day's work "tags along for a ride."

Crew resource management (CRM) is naturally important to make optimal use of all resources in the interest of safety. Patrols of the lines are no less critical a function and situational awareness needs to be maintained at all times by every person aboard. Again, **always**.

Some companies like to say that **it takes at least two to go but only one to say no.** This is a reflection of both the buddy system spirit and respecting even a single member if there is a concern.

Summarizing, one must concur:

- using the proper and tested tools,
- following all safe work practices,
- and communicating any concerns up or down the company organization chart

will keep this work which is more vital now in the grid upgrading and storm damage era than ever before, as safe as it can be made.

Chapter 29

Snake was reading a Justice Department Consent Decree that had him smiling. It always made him smile when a big corporation was forced into doing the right thing after failing to do it on their own.

Billionaire American sports team owners throwing sand in the faces, *in a manner of speaking*, of customers (fans) with physical challenges.

These were the same fans that were spending money at this ballpark to make the billionaire owners and millionaire players even richer. Talk about a face slap!

This decree was against the Chicago Cubs and Wrigley Field who had finally come to agreement on ADA (Americans with Disabilities) deficiencies at their ballpark.

A recent upgrade failed to take ADA into consideration and had failed to provide wheelchair users with seats with adequate sightlines and failed to incorporate wheelchair seating at all into premium clubs and group seating areas.

The agreement will now remedy those failures and for the first time will provide some front-row access for fans in wheelchairs and make modifications to circulation paths that presently restrict many wheelchair-bound patrons at Wrigley Field.

It should not have taken this long to make these changes or taken the involvement of the United States Justice Department, but better late than never thought Snake.

From that news Snake shifted to Mount Olive Township in New Jersey, where a friend of his had contacted him about a long-closed landfill he had worked at, with them, several years back.

Solid-waste landfills weren't the best answer but they were a step closer to better waste management than what he had grown up witnessing. Giant smokestacks were the norm then even in Australia where town rubbish was simply burned with the stacks spewing black smoke day after day for years on end.

Mike had even talked about such a stack just off the Southeast Expressway in Boston that disposed of all of Boston's rubbish in just this manner. A sight he remembered as a young boy travelling in and out of the "big city" with his dad.

That smokestack had been demolished only a few years back serving as a reminder for a decade or two of the foul air polluting practice that was considered at one time to be state-of-the-art waste management.

Sometime in the 70's and 80's the pollution realities of that kind of waste control was realized. But it took places like the Love Canal in upstate New York, to catastrophically fail before the truth of that "waste management" was exposed. Love Canal was a recreational spur canal abandoned when AC current won out over DC current and the canal's hydro potential was no longer called on. As the canal became unused recreationally, serious chemical wastes were dumped there, then once full with thousand s of chemical waste drums, the canal was casually capped with clay and abandoned.

House lots were sold alongside the old canal and before long these same owners were noticing awful smells and chemicals leaching into their yards and basements.

The cleanup was massive and was essentially the first project of the Federal Government's introduction to environmental management in the agency of the newly formed EPA[60] (established by Republican President Richard M. Nixon for some curious trivia).

So the country learned a lot with that debacle and had honestly, like the old commercial, "come a long way baby."

In recent decades the concept of lined, monitored, properly waste-managed landfills throughout America had largely displaced open burning. The burning still allowed necessitated tremendously high heat, stack scrubbers, and close monitoring of allowed emissions.

But most household trash was driven by trash trucks to sealed rubber membrane pits where specialty trucks compacted daily trash and covered it over in a grand scale of construction equipment proficiency but not dissimilar to the trench "cut and cover" hand shovel technology our soldiers used to dispose of their waste back in World War II.

But eventually those pits became mountains and to keep the municipal landfills (what were once called town dumps) from becoming the literal and focal high point of these communities, most were stopped at a conspicuous but not outlandish height. Some featured flares to burn off accumulated methane gas, others allowed the vents to off-gas naturally. After a few years the smell dissipated and the community was left with effectively a massive hill that nobody should really live on. Somewhat of a conundrum for municipal managers have been these many hills.

And this is where the Mount Olive phone call to Cape Safety, Inc.'s Snake Irwin continues.

The good people of Mount Olive had considered a few alternatives for the reuse of their long-closed landfill site.

Maybe a golf course, maybe a strip mall, but few locales wanted to risk breaking the impermeability of their cap to allow foundations for commercial (certainly not residential) development.

How many golf courses did America need and were understood to be selfish reuses of such properties, useful to only a handful of townspeople with the money and leisure to enjoy the game of golf, invariably kept off limits to the non-members at all times?00000

Golf courses, as well, were notorious water users (many would say water wasters) taking lots of gasoline- (fossil fuel) powered mowers to maintain.

Since such hill tops and hill sides were vast, the land invariably had considerable opportunity cost.

Leaving it as a mere multi-acre open area was considered wasteful and an extravagant underuse of a municipal asset that brought no economic assistance back to the community.

Hence, Cape Safety, Inc.'s rather elegant suggestion.

Develop the Combe Landfill site into a solar installation generating clean renewable, carbon-free power. It is a temporary reuse option that can work well on most closed landfill sites.

Solar energy is a great way to transform sites like this and to provide green energy jobs and produce revenue.

The 100-acre Combe site had about 65 acres available for panel deployment for the 25.6 megawatt solar project that would provide clean power for over 4,000 homes and generate tax revenue of about $50,000 annually.

After a landfill closes, a list of post-closure caretaking responsibilities remain for property owners, including maintenance and repair of the cap, leachate removal, and maintaining and monitoring leak detection and groundwater monitoring detection systems.

Having a private ally to assist with these responsibilities can save the municipality even more. These sites now become municipal income centers rather than visual eyesores that encourage citizen misuse.

Although no sites nationally have yet reached the solar plant's 30-year life cycle, when that day comes the panels are recycled and the land can pretty much be returned to its original state. It really is a win-win.

Chapter 30

Most people thought that all these Hollywood and Netflix programs of super villains fighting against the forces of goodness were high level bullshit.

And the way they portrayed those two sides typically confirmed their analysis.

The bad guys really didn't walk like penguins, have twitchy moustaches, have the powers of transformation, or tie young girls to railroad tracks.

The good guys weren't all dashing, invincible, bulletproof, and all knowing either.

Those were stereotypes that would lead one to conclude that high level bullshit was Hollywood's ham handed attempt to define good and bad.

But good and bad existed still. It was simply that both were generally better disguised.

Little organizations like Ekö[61] and Cape Safety, Inc., among hundreds of tiny but equally anonymous "do-gooder" enterprises were the unsung and unknown true good guys; while so many well known conglomerates and big businesses with extraordinarily slick but false advertising budgets were, in every fair evaluation, the planet's bad guys.

But the bad guys usually needed equally bad governmental guys to get what they wanted and that is where the unsung citizen like Batman to the Gotham searchlight, could emerge as a superhero.

Thirteen major companies were responsible for the planet's deforestation. It is coincidentally about the same number as Batman super villains.

A recent analysis by the Zoological Society of London found that over half of the most significant tropical lumber and pulp companies do not publicly commit to protecting biodiversity and only 44% have yet to publicly commit to zero deforestation.

The US-based company **Cargill** has a long history of such destruction and of election interference in many South and Central American countries. They've also aired glowing commercials about themselves forever on Sunday morning news shows touting their commitment to the planet.

Cargill profits handsomely from the destruction of the environment and the exploitation of people.

Their Amazon devastation occurs in Brazil, Argentina, Paraguay, and Bolivia (that they promised to stop by 2025). It looks like the opposite late in 2024 with more plans now for a destructive railway through the rainforest.

Cargill is also notorious for:

- ecosystem, soy and beef production-related devastation in Grand Chaco, and Cerrado;
- In Ghana and Côte d'Ivoire for buying illegally grown coca from public parks;
- In Indonesia and Malaysia for buying palm oil from companies that illegally clear rain forests;
- and for fraudulent accounting that underreports the damage they're doing.

American firms McDonald's, Burger King, Walmart, and Unilever are some of their major customers.

In a final destructive blow to the Amazon, before leaving office, far-right President Jair Bolsonaro, greenlighted construction of a mega-highway that will, if finalized, cut through miles of precious untouched rain forest.

Once built, the road will give illegal loggers and land grabbers easy access to then slash and burn some of the most remote forest areas left in the Amazon—a nightmare to the rainforest and to the indigenous people who still live there. These areas are then used for palm oil plantations.

One recent study estimated that the new highway would cause deforestation to grow by 500% by 2030.

At the very least this project required an honest impact assessment of the consequences of this highway before giant paving companies got underway.

Better yet, a rethink of the entire project.

An unpaved road is in place there now. And unusable only during the wettest months of which fewer are anticipated under climate change inevitability.

So Lars and Sandra thought that they could make that case with their UN contacts. A reasonable concession asking to forego paving out an existing unpaved highway that still serves well the vast majority of those using it.

Maybe they'd get someone in that UN building to see things the planet's way for a change. For far too long the promise of economic expansion being the earth's salvation has been big business's rally song, and for far too long many government's have been singing that song as well.

Business and governments singing for more destruction loudly and proudly while conglomerates steal the country's assets, natural resources, and in many instances the souls and cultures of these countries as well.

Lars looked down the list he was carrying at the other 12 firms with blood on their names regarding their roles in environmental destruction.

Black Rock ranked high for their heavy investment in risky environmental projects including thermal coal. But they were also notorious climate hypocrites with more funding commitments to deforestation efforts than any other fund.

Walmart seemed to be trying but was still the retailer for too many suspiciously sourced products from Cargill and elsewhere. They have done little monitoring of their supply chains.

JBS is one of Brazil's leading exporters of beef and one of the world's biggest meat companies better known as one of the largest deforestation companies in the world. The company even had on its record a conviction for acquiring cattle from a farm in the Brazilian Amazon under sanction for illegal deforestation. Presently trying to go public, their deforestation practices over the past 15 years equal a landmass as large as Ireland.

IKEA was the largest producer of wooden furniture in the world meaning that their operations needed huge amounts of timber, apparently not all designated for felling, or cleared for manufacturing use.

Korindo Group PT is an Indonesia-based producer, processor and manufacturer of various products, including wind towers, battery separators, specialized container vehicles, and cast iron products. It also has plantations of palm oil and timber. Korindo has engaged in massive scale deforestation in Papua and North Maluku Indonesia and has been using the FSC's eco-forestry label to greenwash its practices. An investigation of them found that the company destroys critical wildlife habitats and violates human rights. It sells timber, pulpwood, plywood, newsprint, and biomass to Asia and Australia.

Starbucks is the largest chain of coffee shops in the world with over 24,000 outlets in 70 countries. Its sourcing commitment has been abysmal particularly as relates to palm oil, soy, and pulp and paper. A *Wall Street Journal* investigation found human rights abuses on plantations in Malaysia. The company also has a horrific reputation for ratifying with any shops that have decided to unionize.

McDonald's with 36,000 locations in 100 countries uses over 120,000 metric tons of palm oil sourced through Cargill, the leading deforestation conglomerate.

Yum! Brands has not eliminated deforestation from its supply chains and did not even meet industry-wide deforestation goals.

Ahold Delhaize that forms a conglomerate umbrella over such supermarket chains as Stop and Shop, Food Lion, Giant, Hannaford among others claimed deforestation objectives would be met by 2025 but in 2018 they launched a $100 million joint venture with Cargill to operate a new meat packing plant for its own stores and JBS.

Procter and Gamble the consumer goods giant was given a grade of **F** in a scorecard released by Rainforest Action Network when evaluating major firms involved in deforestation. Their infringement on indigenous rights and threatened species is also well documented.

The battle against these conglomerates was a worthy one that CSI believed most of their fellow planet dwellers were in agreement with. So the daily news surrounding Halloween season where their planet mates were more the culprits than giant conglomerates truly annoyed Sue Mei in the west coast.

"Come on, people," she said in an exacerbated voice, "do better."

Her attitude was all about the plight and flight of small painted woolly bats.

The bats were selfless little forest guardians, helping to control pests and pollinate flowers – but a sick Halloween trinkets trend was fueling demand for their bodies.

Suddenly they're being kidnapped from their forest homes across south and south-east Asia, their dead bodies sold as frivolous Halloween decorations on platforms like Amazon and eBay.

Horrifyingly, thought Sue, the demand from the US appeared to be the biggest threat to the species' survival!

"Damn our own people sometimes, we know better," Sue said out loud this time. It broke the slumber of Toughie the cat. "Did we learn nothing from the old dime store good luck charms of rabbits' feet?" Toughie, sneezed, a sure sign of agreement.

"We can turn this around."

Etsy had already banned the sale of bats. Good for them. Now Sue had the chance to take this pressure further and demand Amazon and eBay follow suit to stop this grotesque trinket trade.

A phone call and discussion to a few newspaper journalists and social media influencers she had as contacts could get the two companies' attention. Maybe a phone call to Rachel and Ali V at MSNBC would help, too.

She knew those two companies would only act if they could feel the heat from tens of thousands of mad customers around the world.

It was a little macabre thinking that Amazon and eBay were awash with the bodies of these little bats, some sold as jewelry or stuffed in jars.

These stunning creatures known for their flaming orange and black wings are at particular risk of dying out because they reproduce so slowly, just one offspring at a time.

But if Sue could build enough pressure on Amazon and eBay to stop selling them, demand for these creatures would take a massive hit and they could finally start to recover in the wild.

At a time when species are disappearing at alarming speed, we have to do everything we can to save the precious wildlife we have left.

Ironic that Sue would be spending any energy on as off-the-mission a subject as this but every day it was becoming more and more apparent how interconnected was man and the animal world.

West Nile virus remained a concern in newspapers, and Dr. Anthony Fauci, the leading American physician-scientist and immunologist who served as the director of the National Institute of Allergy and Infectious Diseases from 1984 to 2022, and the chief medical advisor to the president from 2021 to 2022, had just recovered from a serious West Nile virus that threatened to take his life.

It can literally happen to the best of us.

So what do bats eat? Well, contrary to the claims of bats devouring 1,000 mosquitoes per hour, a more grounded reality unfolds from a study by the University of Wisconsin. While bats can eat mosquitoes, they tend not to dominate their diet. But bats help control mosquitoes. That was a fact.

But Sue noted that these UW researchers revealed that mosquitoes were found in 72% of little brown bat fecal samples, astonishingly higher than previous estimates.

Proof, that somehow all of the earth's creatures play a role on this planet.

Sue also gave a tip of the hat to any researcher who could identify that 72% of a bat dropping was mosquito in composition.

"That's batshit wild," she said once again to Toughie, who missed the joke entirely.

"I need a better audience," she admitted.

Chapter 31

Claus, with just a hint of a German accent turned his head in the same way that Sergeant Shultz, the character on the old TV show, Hogan's Heroes once did then paused in the same confused manner, and uttered, "I know nuth ◊ think."

China's Ministry of State Security had just announced that it has found various spying devices on the oceans' surface and deep seas, including advanced underwater "lighthouses" allegedly used to help foreign submarines.

The government said these devices were hidden on the ocean floor and transmitting data about China's territorial waters.

In typical Chinese hyperbole their announcement stated that some devices acted as "secret agents," drifting with ocean currents to monitor activities in real-time, while others functioned as underwater "lighthouses," directing foreign submarines in Chinese seas.

The specifics of where these devices were found were not revealed, but the ministry said they were located in areas claimed by China.

Of course that was the constant rub between China and the rest of the world. China had been in a form of cold war territory grab for years now redefining what were understood as international waters as their own through island and atoll land grabs that would then extend the mileage of their "territorial waters" and "economic zone" into sea lanes that ships had travelled freely for years.

In recent years American naval vessels, Philippine naval vessels, non-Chinese fishing and even commercial vessels had been fire hosed, intercepted, and otherwise harassed, by Chinese Coast Guard and naval ships sailing through the same waters they had sailed through for decades.

The announcement only amplified China's accusations of continuous foreign surveillance in its maritime territories.

The South China Sea is a crucial area due to its rich natural resources and important maritime routes, and disputes over these waters have only increased geopolitical tensions.

Recent disputes between China and the Philippines have raised concerns about a possible conflict that might involve the United States, which has a mutual defense treaty with the Philippines.

The U.S. Navy often conducts operations in the South China Sea, a move which China sees as provocative. The ministry's statement about the spying devices could worsen these tensions, as China may take action against alleged foreign snooping. But defense analysts believed that undersea "lighthouses" could improve foreign military capabilities by providing detailed navigation assistance in contested waters.

The Philippines has expressed its concerns over China's actions, particularly the deployment of Chinese vessels in its exclusive economic zone. Filipino officials have described these actions as "coercive," showing aggression with Chinese maritime practices.

Maybe it all related to China's Taiwan ambitions. China continues to have serious concerns about Taiwan since it considers the self-governing island to be a part of its territory. While Beijing's claims did not specify which nations may be behind the deployment of these spy devices, the Chinese government is concerned about foreign espionage activity in the region.

Cape Safety, Inc. had been working with both the U.S. Coast Guard and U.S. Navy in several capacities recently and for three days, a few months back, Claus' whereabouts on the company deployment board was simply listed as, ***Washington - Undefined***.

It wasn't the first time a consultant's deployment had been shrouded, even in-house, but the timing based on this Chinese Press Release was curious.

"So if I asked you to describe the lunchroom in the Pentagon, you'd be flummoxed?" kidded Snake, over another of East Sweepster's bakery delights.

"Lunchroom, Pentagon, Washington,—I've heard those words before but really can't say more," said Claus with a smile.

Snake knew enough to drop the topic with a smile of his own.

It was another headline with more international intrigue, of a sort.

Who were those anonymous, yet everyday folks, that were helping the United States remain safe day after day?

Chapter 32

Jeremy was on the lookout for a warm winter jacket to get through another cold New England winter so the local L.L. Bean outlet in Mashpee Commons was a sure place to start.

But the highest quality coats, jackets, even comforters and other insulated products available depressed him greatly.

He thought the store was better than this.

Despite the many high-quality alternatives available, the iconic Maine outerwear store, L.L. Bean, was still retailing products with down – the soft layer of feathers closest to a bird's skin.

Jeremy had seen the process and it wasn't kind or necessary. Workers literally stepped on live birds' fragile necks or delicate wings and rip out their feathers so forcefully it often tears their skin open.

The birds may endure this terrifying ordeal up to 15 times before they're violently killed.

Every down-filled jacket, pillow, and sleeping bag comes from a duck or goose that was tortured, neglected, and slaughtered. Ducks and geese bred for their feathers and flesh are often packed by the thousands into dark, filthy sheds. Birds exploited by the meat industry are rapidly fattened to meet the target slaughter weight, which usually leads to joint inflammation, broken legs, respiratory issues, and heart failure.

At a duck slaughterhouse, investigators who were known to Jeremy had even filmed a worker violently grabbing and stepping on ducks and shackling them upside down. Then, the hanging birds were dragged through an electrified bath that paralyzed them but left them conscious. The worker then stabbed them in the neck and left the birds dangling and bleeding out. Many of the birds moved for more than a minute afterwards.

On farms visited by PETA Asia, ducks were packed into filthy sheds and forced to stand on wire flooring or confined to dirt lots covered in feces. Investigators found that birds were denied the opportunity to bathe, swim, fly, or forage. Many were gasping for air or suffering from wounds, and some struggled to walk or even stand.

Dying birds were neglected, and dead birds were often left to decompose among the living. Each of the farms and slaughterhouses investigated by PETA Asia was certified by the bogus Responsible Down Standard.

No one needs to wear feathers stolen from tormented birds to stay warm.

Widely available ethical options for staying cozy include cotton, viscose, Lyocell, polyester, and new materials like PrimaLoft, Thermal R, and kapok.

Jeremy would definitely be picking one of these ethical options instead and L.L. Bean even carried a line of Polar fleece products made from recycled plastic bottles that began in Lawrence, MA, at a textile plant called Malden Mills.

"Where is that fleece department?" he asked a clerk.

William and Jeremy had picked out a perfect spot on the complex, near the landing pad and overlooking Martha's Vineyard. They had the sign made on four pink marble slabs that would be mounted for all to read as a touchstone for the firm's future employees and friends.

The next monthly meeting they would pull off the white tarpaulin they had placed over it temporarily to maintain the mystery. The rest of the staff didn't know about it, and even Sandra, Mike and Lars were in the dark as to what the actual message would be.

But William traced his fingers across the lettering as Jeremy stood back approvingly at the pledge, now written in stone.

Really, written in stone:

ENGINEERS CODE OF CONDUCT

Engineers shall conduct themselves honorably, responsibly, ethically, and lawfully so as to enhance the honor, reputation, and usefulness of the profession

Epilogue

Nathaniel Philbrick in his book, *Travels with George*, quoted a concern of George Washington that he found far too prophetic in times like we live in now. I, too, found it too valuable to leave in dusty archives not to be pondered and maybe quoted relating to present day.

He was writing about what could happen to America if a President's chief priority became to divide us rather than unite us:

> "It serves always to distract the public councils and enfeeble the public administration.
>
> It agitates the community with ill-founded jealousies and false alarms, kindles the animosity of one part against another, and foments occasionally riot and insurrection.
>
> It opens the door to foreign influence and corruption, which finds a facilitated access to the government itself through the channels of party passions.
>
> Thus the policy and will of one country are subjected to the policy and will of another."

On November 5, 2024, the citizens of the United States of America voted to return
Donald Trump and his regime to the White House.
THE END

OTHER BOOKS FROM WAQUOIT WORDSMITH PRESS:

Non-fiction:
An iGen Cookbook for the Unskilled by Lavinia M. Hughes
Deep Sea Decisions by Richard Hughes

Fiction:
Enter Through the Crawlspace by Lavinia M. Hughes
Enter Through the Bulkhead by Lavinia M. Hughes
Enter Through the Alleyway by Lavinia M. Hughes
Enter Through the Porthole by Lavinia M. Hughes

Newtucket Island by Richard Hughes and Lavinia M. Hughes
Training Ship by Richard Hughes and Lavinia M. Hughes
Cape Car Blues by Richard Hughes and Lavinia M. Hughes
Mikey Mayflower—the Early Years by Richard Hughes and Lavinia M. Hughes

Cape Safety, Inc. — by Richard Hughes (Danger Dogs Series #1)
Cape Safety, Inc. — *Cast of Characters* by Richard Hughes (Danger Dogs Series #2)
Cape Safety, Inc. — *Where Problems Perish* by Richard Hughes (Danger Dogs Series #3)
Cape Safety, Inc. — *Still Standing* by Richard Hughes (Danger Dogs Series #4)
Cape Safety, Inc. — *Change of Climate* by Richard Hughes (Danger Dogs Series #5)
Cape Safety, Inc. — *S.H.E.* by Richard Hughes (Danger Dogs Series #6)
Cape Safety, Inc. — *New Blood* by Richard Hughes (Danger Dogs Series #7)
Cape Safety, Inc. — *Humanity Minders* by Richard Hughes (Danger Dogs Series #8)
Cape Safety, Inc. — *The New Guard* (Danger Dogs Series #9)
Cape Safety, Inc.—*Sawbuck Safety* (Danger Dogs Series #10)

---

[1] The DOJ has indicted TENET Media for taking Russian money in order to influence the 2024 election. The DOJ's indictment The DOJ has indicted TENET Media for taking Russian money in order to influence the 2024 election. The DOJ's

indictment states TENET Media hired pro-Trump personalities as part of their operation. The media company hired Tim Pool, Benny Johnson, Dave Rubin, Lauren Southern, Tayler Hansen, and others. MeidasTouch has also uncovered that Trump amplified content from TENET media personalities multiple times.

[2] Both by number of stations and by revenue. The 855 stations reach more than 110 million listeners every week, and 276 million every month.

[3] Audacy Corp. filed for Chapter 11 bankruptcy in the United States District Court for the Southern District of Texas[1] on January 7, 2024 (case no. 24-90024), along with 47 affiliated companies. The law firm Porter Hedges, LLP is representing the firm. The bankruptcy petition lists assets and liabilities of more than $1 billion and the number of creditors between 5,000 and 10,000.[2]2 A month later, it received court approval for a reorganization plan that will allow it to emerge from bankruptcy once the plan receives regulatory approval from the Federal Communications Commission.

[4] The **hunter versus farmer hypothesis** is a proposed explanation for the nature of attention-deficit hyperactivity disorder (ADHD). It was first suggested by radio host Thom Hartmann in his book *Attention Deficit Disorder: A Different Perception*. The hypothesis notes that humans spent most of their evolutionary history in hunter-gatherer societies, and it argues that ADHD represents a lack of adaptation to farming societies. Hartmann first developed the idea as a mental model after his own son was diagnosed with ADHD, stating, "It's not hard science, and was never intended to be."

[5] On its very baseline **creative nonfiction** is a literary genre. Some people call it the fourth genre, along with **poetry, fiction** and **drama**. And it's an umbrella term for the many different ways one can write what is called **creative nonfiction**.

[6] https://injuryfacts.nsc.org/work/costs/work-injury-costs/

[7] Of course, that is only after they swim through the razor wire positioned in the waters of the Rio Grande that Texas Governor Abbott heartlessly placed there to slice up, men, women, even children, attempting to cross this river for better lives.

[8] *Cape Safety, Inc. - Sawbuck Safety*, Book #10 by Richard Hughes

[9] The history of the United States Army Corps of Engineers can be traced back to the American Revolution[3]. On 16 June 1775, the Continental Congress[4]

---

1. https://en.wikipedia.org/wiki/United_States_District_Court_for_the_Southern_District_of_Texas
2. https://en.wikipedia.org/wiki/Audacy#cite_note-2

organized the Corps of Engineers, whose initial staff included a chief engineer[5] and two assistants.[6][6] Colonel[7] Richard Gridley[8] became General George Washington[9]'s first chief engineer. One of his first tasks was to build fortifications near Boston[10] at Bunker Hill[11]. The Continental Congress recognized the need for engineers trained in military fortifications and asked the government of King Louis XVI[12] of France for assistance. Many of the early engineers in the Continental Army were former French officers.

[10] Lucian K. Truscott IV, Substack, 14 years old

[11] Generic version of Pseudoephedrine

[12] *Gun Country* by Andrew C. McKevitt and *The Hidden History of Guns and the Second Amendment* by Thom Hartmann

[13] The prior election Representatives Mike Collins and Marjorie Taylor Greene each had television commercials featuring them with the identical AR-15 weapon, actually shooting voting machines as their apparent solution to Georgia gun violence. Somehow voters agreed with them.

[14] Maine Belon Oysters are a rare and highly sought-after oyster variety that is native to Europe and were introduced to Maine in the 1950s. Belon Oysters are the European Flat species (Ostrea edulis) and are known for their distinctive flavor and texture.

[15] National Fire Protection Association, Quincy, MA

[16] **Petrography** is a branch of petrology[13] that focuses on detailed descriptions of rocks[14]. Someone who studies petrography is called a **petrographer**. The mineral[15] content and the textural[16] relationships within the rock are described in detail. The

3.	https://en.wikipedia.org/wiki/American_Revolution
4.	https://en.wikipedia.org/wiki/Continental_Congress
5.	https://en.wikipedia.org/wiki/Chief_of_Engineers
6.	https://en.wikipedia.org/wiki/United_States_Army_Corps_of_Engineers#cite_note-history-6
7.	https://en.wikipedia.org/wiki/Colonel_(United_States)
8.	https://en.wikipedia.org/wiki/Richard_Gridley
9.	https://en.wikipedia.org/wiki/George_Washington
10.	https://en.wikipedia.org/wiki/Boston
11.	https://en.wikipedia.org/wiki/Bunker_Hill_Monument
12.	https://en.wikipedia.org/wiki/Louis_XVI_of_France
13.	https://en.wikipedia.org/wiki/Petrology
14.	https://en.wikipedia.org/wiki/Rock_(geology)
15.	https://en.wikipedia.org/wiki/Mineral
16.	https://en.wikipedia.org/wiki/Rock_microstructure

CAPE SAFETY, INC. - EVENTS WON'T STOP 217

classification of rocks[17] is based on the information acquired during the **petrographic analysis**.

[17] consisting of or containing a pun or puns

[18] Pocfpride.com, on Instagram @megan.waldrep

[19] Emergency Position-Indicating Radio Beacon

[20] Naloxone is an opioid antagonist[18]: a medication[19] used to reverse or reduce[20] the effects of opioids[21]. For example, it is used to restore breathing after an opioid overdose[22]. Effects begin within two minutes.

---

17. https://en.wikipedia.org/wiki/Rock_(geology)

18. https://www.bing.com/ck/

    a?!&&p=e076a1c78aa895b7JmltdHM9MTcyNzIyMjQwMCZpZ3VpZD0zNTc0MDQyNi1jNDI0LTZhOWMt MDQ3MS0xMDFlYzUwNDZiZjkmaW5zaWQ9NTkxNA&ptn=3&ver=2&hsh=3&fclid=35740426-c424-6a9c-0471-101ec5046bf9&u=a1L3NlYXJjaD9xPU9waW9pZCUyMGFudGFnb25pc3QlMjB3aWtpcGVkaWEmZm9ybT1XSUtJUkU&ntb=1

19. https://www.bing.com/ck/

    a?!&&p=dc0c1236245957beJmltdHM9MTcyNzIyMjQwMCZpZ3VpZD0zNTc0MDQyNi1jNDI0LTZhOWMt MDQ3MS0xMDFlYzUwNDZiZjkmaW5zaWQ9NTkxNQ&ptn=3&ver=2&hsh=3&fclid=35740426-c424-6a9c-0471-101ec5046bf9&u=a1L3NlYXJjaD9xPU1lZGljYXRpb24lMjB3aWtpcGVkaWEmZm9ybT1XSUtJUkU&ntb=1

20. https://www.bing.com/ck/

    a?!&&p=e6652e5b76dad646JmltdHM9MTcyNzIyMjQwMCZpZ3VpZD0zNTc0MDQyNi1jNDI0LTZhOWMt MDQ3MS0xMDFlYzUwNDZiZjkmaW5zaWQ9NTkxNg&ptn=3&ver=2&hsh=3&fclid=35740426-c424-6a9c-0471-101ec5046bf9&u=a1L3NlYXJjaD9xPVJlY2VwdG9yJTIwYW50YWdvbmlzdCUyMHdpa2lwZWRpYSZmb3JtPVdJS0lSRQ&ntb=1

21. https://www.bing.com/ck/

    a?!&&p=589273c33bc28ea4JmltdHM9MTcyNzIyMjQwMCZpZ3VpZD0zNTc0MDQyNi1jNDI0LTZhOWMt MDQ3MS0xMDFlYzUwNDZiZjkmaW5zaWQ9NTkxNw&ptn=3&ver=2&hsh=3&fclid=35740426-c424-6a9c-0471-101ec5046bf9&u=a1L3NlYXJjaD9xPU9waW9pZHMlMjB3aWtpcGVkaWEmZm9ybT1XSUtJUkU&ntb=1

22. https://www.bing.com/ck/

    a?!&&p=d32e28a596ab2e53JmltdHM9MTcyNzIyMjQwMCZpZ3VpZD0zNTc0MDQyNi1jNDI0LTZhOWMt MDQ3MS0xMDFlYzUwNDZiZjkmaW5zaWQ9NTkxOA&ptn=3&ver=2&hsh=3&fclid=35740426-c424-6a9c-0471-101ec5046bf9&u=a1L3NlYXJjaD9xPU9waW9pZCUyMG92ZXJkb3NlJTIwd2lraXBlZGlhJmZvcm09V0lLSVJF&ntb=1

[21] Amsea.org/training or amsea.org/commercial fishermen

[22] British spelling

[23] This **phrase** is still common in **Ireland**, even today. It is used to describe either someone who has some serious charm when it comes to their speech or to describe someone who just does not know when to shut up.

[24] *I Heard There Was A Secret Chord* by Daniel J, Levitin, 2024, W.W. Norton & Co.

[25] The phrase "ridden hard and put away wet" is an idiom that originates from the southern and western United States[23][24]. It is used to describe someone who looks worn out or exhausted after a long day's work, similar to a horse that has been ridden hard without proper care[25][26].

[26] A **statutory harbour authority** (**SHA**) is a designated body that has been given **statutory powers or duties** for the purpose of improving, maintaining, or managing a harbor[27]. These authorities are responsible for **safety, efficiency, and environmental protection** within their jurisdiction[28].

[27] Dr. Oliver Sacks, the elder statesman for people with neurological differences, has suggested that different brain chemistry might be a requirement for creativity. And one of the world's top neuroscientists, Dr. Richard Silberstein, has even published a brilliant paper[29] drawing a direct and positive correlation between ADHD and creativity. Thom Hartmann reported that many of the people who shared their stories for me to publish in *Hunters in a Farmer's World* said that expressing their creativity was an important part of their lives and helped with building and maintaining their self-esteem.

[28] This quote, "If you want something done, ask a busy person," is a somewhat paradoxical statement suggesting that busy people are more likely to get things done than those who are not. This might seem counterintuitive at first glance, as one might

23. https://www.languagehumanities.org/what-does-rode-hard-and-put-away-wet-mean.htm
24. **https://www.languagehumanities.org/what-does-rode-hard-and-put-away-wet-mean.htm**
25. https://crossidioms.com/ridden-hard-and-put-away-wet/
26. **https://crossidioms.com/ridden-hard-and-put-away-wet/**
27. https://en.wikipedia.org/wiki/Competent_harbour_authority
28. https://www.hayesparsons.co.uk/what-is-a-harbour-authority/
29. https://substack.com/redirect/228bab90-d40a-402e-a934-01ae96470dd8?j=eyJ1IjoiMTZmaTEifQ.hfUh4MHjC5u1Q41pcLsRxmtE9Qp-h-1bkSNV4ufuOcE

think that a person with less on their plate would have more time[30] and energy to devote to a new task. However, the underlying principle here is that busy people are often more organized, efficient, and skilled at managing their time. They have to be in order to handle their existing workload. Therefore, they are more likely to find a way to fit in an additional task and complete it successfully.

[29] *Cattle Ships*: Being The Fifth Chapter Of Mr. Plimsoll's *Second Appeal For Our Seamen* By Samuel Plimsoll[31]. This work has been selected by scholars as being culturally important, and is part of the knowledge base of civilization as we know it.

[30] *The RTÉ Investigates, Live Exports: On the Hoof*, was aired on October 8, 2024.

[31] *Chicken*, Steve Schriffler and *Cape Safety, Inc. - Humanity Minders*, by Richard Hughes.

[32] *The Soul of an Octopus* by Sy Montgomery for one.

[33] Dutch marine services company Boskalis has embarked on the final phase of a 15-month saga involving the car carrier formerly known as *Fremantle Highway*[32]. The car carrier was fully loaded with vehicles, including hundreds of electric vehicles, when it suffered a devastating fire in the North Sea off the coast of the Netherlands in July 2023. The blaze claimed one crew member's life and left seven others injured as they desperately jumped overboard to escape the flames.

A team from Boskalis' SMIT Salvage, alongside partner Multraship, provided the salvage response to the emergency. "We successfully stabilized the vessel, brought the fire under control, and the car carrier was then towed to Eemshaven where the salvage team carried out essential quayside work," the company said. In October 2024, its 275-meter long *BOKA Vanguard*, the world's largest semi-submersible heavy lift vessel, loaded the unrecognizable hulk onto its expansive deck at the Port of Rotterdam. The cargo will be secured for a long voyage to the Far East, where it will undergo further repairs and modifications before returning to service.

---

30. https://quotes.guide/about/time/

31. https://www.thriftbooks.com/a/samuel-plimsoll/562659/

32. *https://gcaptain.com/tag/fremantle-highway/*

[34] *Junior Mints, golf balls, and leather jackets: 20 things still made in Massachusetts*, Oct 15, 2024, Scott Kirsner, Globe Correspondent

[35] A platinum flute with sterling silver mechanism was commissioned for the 1939 World's Fair in New York. This flute was owned and played by the famous flutist William Kincaid until shortly before his death in 1967. In 1986 this flute was auctioned by Christie's for $170,000 plus $17,000 for the auction house fee, the highest price ever paid for a flute.

[36] The term 'Fore' originated as "fore-caddie" in Scotland and has evolved into a vital part of golf's safety protocol and etiquette. The fore rule is one of the oldest rules in golf. It is believed to have originated in the 18th century, when golfers would shout "fore" to warn each other of approaching balls. The rule was formalized in the 1890s, and it has been in place ever since.

[37] IUCN Redlist, 2024

[38] The Luddites were members of a 19th-century movement of English textile workers who opposed the use of certain types of automated machinery due to concerns relating to worker pay and output quality. They often destroyed the machines in organized raids. Members of the group referred to themselves as Luddites, self-described followers of "Ned Ludd", a legendary weaver whose name was used as a pseudonym in threatening letters to mill owners and government officials.

[39] Devin Liddell, a futurist at Teague

[40] Ph. D.

[41] *Slavery and Abolitionism on Cape Cod* by Michael V. Pregot

[42] *Cape Safety, Inc.- Humanity Minders*, Book #8 by Richard Hughes, Chapter 25

[43] Oceannews.com

[44] New York and New Jersey have resources for anyone experiencing mental health crises, including those considering suicide. You can reach the National Suicide & Crisis Lifeline any time by calling or texting 988, or by chatting online[33], to be connected for free local mental health resources and emergency counselors. Health officials advise anyone observing warning signs[34] of suicidal ideation to call for help or take the person to an emergency room for immediate care.

[45] The **monkey's fist** knot is most often used as the weight in a heaving **line**. The **line** would have the **monkey's fist** on one end, an eye splice or bowline on the other, with about 30 feet (~10 metres) of line between. A lightweight feeder **line** would be

---

33. https://chat.988lifeline.org/

34. https://njhopeline.com/faq/

tied to the bowline, then the weighted heaving **line** could be hurled between ship and dock.

[46] Restech PLT®

[47] Velella is a monospecific genus of hydrozoa in the Porpitidae family. Its only known species is Velella velella, a cosmopolitan free-floating hydrozoan that lives on the surface of the open ocean. It is commonly known by the names sea raft, by-the-wind sailor, purple sail, little sail, or simply Velella.

[48] **Deferred Action for Childhood Arrivals (DACA)** is a United States immigration policy[35]. It allows some individuals who, on June 15, 2012, were physically present in the United States with no lawful immigration status after having entered the country as children at least five years earlier, to receive a renewable two-year period of deferred action[36] from deportation[37] and to be eligible for an employment authorization document[38] (work permit[39]).

[49] Ekō is a community of people from around the world committed to curbing the growing power of corporations. We want to buy from, work for and invest in companies that respect the environment, treat their workers well and respect democracy. And we're not afraid to hold them to account when they don't.

Barely a day goes by without a fresh corporate scandal making headlines. From polluting the environment to dodging taxes – when left unchecked, corporations don't let anything stand in the way of bigger profits.

In an age of multinational companies that are bigger and richer than some countries, it can be easy to feel powerless. But they have a weakness. The biggest corporations in the world rely on ordinary people to keep them in business. We are their customers, their employees, and often their investors. When we act together, we can be more powerful than they are. Together, our community of millions act as a global consumer watchdog – running and winning campaigns to hold the biggest companies in the world accountable.

[50] The United States Court of Appeals' 2–1 ruling means SeaWorld trainers will continue to be **prohibited** from entering the water with whales during shows, eliminating the dives, jumps, and many other tricks.

[51] The **WDC Whale and Dolphin Conservation** (us.whales.org/our-goals/end-captivity/orca-captivity/) group maintained a web page with a running tally,

---

35. https://en.wikipedia.org/wiki/United_States_immigration_policy
36. https://en.wikipedia.org/wiki/Deferred_action
37. https://en.wikipedia.org/wiki/Deportation
38. https://en.wikipedia.org/wiki/Employment_authorization_document
39. https://en.wikipedia.org/wiki/Work_permit

presently indicating 55 orcas held in captivity, 22 were captured in the wild, and 33 were born in captivity. Their vision statement read: *Our vision of a world where every whale and dolphin is safe and free is not a noble gesture, but an essential means to sustain the future of our earth by increasing the planet's climate resiliency.*

[52] Roughly half of the world's cobalt reserves[40] are found in the resource-rich earth of the Democratic Republic Congo—one of the poorest countries on the planet. Nearly three-quarters of the global supply of mined cobalt comes from just two Congolese provinces, Haut-Katanga and Lualaba, in what's known as the Central African Copperbelt.

In the DRC's artisanal mining sector[41]—which exists alongside the formal mining industry—children and adults toil underground for hours in dangerous tunnels, using sticks or makeshift tools to mine for the cobalt-rich mineral heterogenite. Others sift ore in noxious, contaminated waters. With no protective equipment, injuries and deaths[42] are common. Their take-home pay at the end of the day is often less than $2.

The human and environmental destruction[43] caused by mining in the DRC is staggering. Entire communities have been forced to leave their homes to make way for a new mining concession. Toxic waste has contaminated critical water sources and arable land. Millions of trees have been razed. The air, hazy with dust and particulates from open-pit mines, is dangerous to breathe.

These inhumane working conditions, environmental harms, and the exploitative companies that underpin the deadly global cobalt trade[44] aren't a recent phenomenon in the DRC. From the rubber farms of King Leopold's brutal Congo Free State in the 1890s to the palm oil plantations and uranium mines of the twentieth century, cobalt mining is just the latest chapter in a centuries-long story of exploitation in the DRC.

[53] *A Sea Full of Turtles*, by Bill Streever

[54] Congress added a new provision in the Violence Against Women Reauthorization Act of 2022. This lets you bring a civil action in federal court against someone who shared intimate images, explicit pictures, recorded videos, or other depictions of you without your consent (15 U.S.C. § 6851). It also includes sharing

---

40. https://www.statista.com/statistics/264930/global-cobalt-reserves/

41. https://www.pactworld.org/blog/artisanal-miners-hidden-critical-force-global-economy

42. https://www.wilsoncenter.org/blog-post/drc-mining-industry-child-labor-and-formalization-small-scale-mining

43. https://earth.org/cobalt-mining-in-congo/

44. https://www.cfr.org/blog/why-cobalt-mining-drc-needs-urgent-attention

those intimate images through technology, such as the internet or social media. Source: United States Department of Justice web page.

[55] For more on the philosophy of how designers destroyed the world and what can be done to fix it, read *Ruined by Design*, by Mike Monteiro.

[56] Dr. Anuvitha Kamath says that Norovirus, also known as Norwalk Virus, is a contagious virus that causes severe vomiting and diarrhea. This virus belongs to a group of calciviridae. It causes inflammation of the stomach and intestine walls. The symptoms of this are stomach pain, nausea, vomiting, diarrhea (loose stools), fever, body aches, and headache. The symptoms usually appear after 12 to 48 hours of exposure to the virus and last for about 2 to 3 days. The treatment for this is drinking plenty of fluids to prevent dehydration, eating a soft bland diet, and taking adequate rest.

[57] *Cape Safety, Inc. - Sawbuck Safety*, Book #10 Chapter 29, by Richard Hughes

[58] *The Dangerous Case of Donald Trump* by Bandy Lee, M.D.

[59] *The Demon of Unrest*, by Erik Larsen

[60] Environmental Protection Agency

[61] Ekö is a worldwide movement of people like you, working together to hold corporations accountable for their actions forging a new sustainable path for our global economy.

Don't miss out!

Visit the website below and you can sign up to receive emails whenever Richard Hughes publishes a new book. There's no charge and no obligation.

https://books2read.com/r/B-A-MSLF-LJNIF

BOOKS 2 READ

Connecting independent readers to independent writers.

About the Author

Richard Hughes closed his 24-seat safety training center on Cape Cod to become a retired student of modern worldwide shipping operations. He graduated from Massachusetts Maritime Academy with a B.S. in Marine Transportation then obtained a Masters Degree in Business from Lesley University. While at MMA, he sailed on the *Bay State*, the *Lightning*, and the *Mobil Lube*. His books include the **Cape Safety, Inc. – Danger Dogs Series**—a collection of 11 novels detailing the exciting lives of a top-notch bi-coastal safety consulting firm. His popular non-fiction **Deep Sea Decisions** is an expose of maritime tragedies. He and his wife, Lavinia M. Hughes, have co-authored **Newtucket Island, Training Ship, Cape Car Blues** and **Mikey Mayflower - The Early Years**. He lives and writes in the seaside village of Waquoit, MA, with his wife.

About the Publisher

Waquoit Wordsmith Press is located in the seaside village of Waquoit in Falmouth, Massachusetts.

Cover Design by author Richard Hughes